BELLS ON HER TOES

PSYCHIC SEASONS

BOOK TWO

REGINA WELLING

Bells on Her Toes

ISBN- 978-1-953044-28-0

Cover art by: L. Vryhof
Interior design by: L. Vryhof

www.reginawelling.com

First Edition
Printed in the U.S.A.

Table of Contents

Chapter One

One year ago

And they lived happily ever after.

Okay, so maybe what the author actually said was that the couple happily climbed into bed together, but Gustavia Roman knew the happily ever after was implied. Or was it inferred? She sometimes got those two words mixed up.

Picking up her cup of herbal tea, she inhaled its minty, green scent then savored a mouthful before turning off her E-reader.

It's funny, she thought, how the bad guys from fairy tales have been replaced by the mundane trials of life in contemporary stories. Death, finances and ego have all ousted the evil queen. At least the prince was still handsome and sometimes even charming.

Hopefully her prince would come along soon. Honestly, he didn't have to be a prince; she could be just as happy with a frog as long as he had certain attributes. He had to be fun, stable, articulate, good with kids and, hey, there was nothing wrong with wishing for a guy with a great body. Oh, and he had to be willing to dance. Gustavia loved to dance. He didn't even have to be good at it, just so long as he got out there and moved around a little.

In order to put her desire out into the universe, Gustavia selected a nice white pillar candle and selecting the fingernail cleaning utensil from her manicure kit, carved her frog prince's description into it. Then, she lit the candle to send her wish wafting into the ether. Trusting that she had done her part to set the gears in motion she continued on with her morning routine.

Pulling on a pair of yoga pants and a loose, cotton tee that said, *Cereal Killer* across the front, she stepped into the peaceful oasis of her backyard garden. Sunflowers lined the fenced in border of her property, towering over plantings of vibrantly colored lilies, larkspur and Iris. Two mature trees, an oak and a maple, cast dappled pools of shade for those plants that like to keep their feet cool in the summer.

In addition to floral plantings, she'd added beds of vegetables and herbs, enough to fill her table with good things to eat.

Off to the left stood a little potting shed surrounded by peonies, a few late bloomers still blossoming, their blood red heads bowed down by their own weight scenting the air. Created out of reclaimed materials, she and her best friend Julie had built the shed, roofing it with a sheet of corrugated metal that played heavenly music when it rained. Plastic barrels, also reclaimed and faux painted to look like weathered wood held rainwater to be used for dry weather irrigation.

This year's project would be an outdoor, solar rainwater shower. She'd already picked up a long, coiled length of black plastic tubing and attached it to the roof of the potting shed. One end she fitted with a large funnel mounted on a stand she'd found at the Salvation Army that had only needed a slight modification to work for her intended purpose. On the other end of the tubing, she used several plumbing adapters to fit it out with a shower head. The coiled tubing, filled by the funnel when it rained, heated by the sun, held enough water for a decent shower and was plenty warm. The only thing left to finish the project was to add an enclosure and some sort of drainage system that would divert the water into one of the flower beds. No use in wasting it.

She liked the satisfaction of creating, building something from nothing and by using recycled materials; she did her part to reduce waste. It was a complete win, in her opinion.

After making the rounds with her clippers and throwing the dead heads into the compost pile, Gustavia chose a spot near a hedge of fragrant roses and began her workout with a sun salutation. Then, she ramped it up by running through a series of Krav Maga moves that left her feeling toned and full of energy. The combination of peaceful stretches and aggressive kicks, punches and spins, she felt, balanced her out, prepared her for whatever the day might bring. As always, she hoped for peace but prepared for war.

"EMBER CIRCLED the village three times, dipping his wings at his new friends below. He was sad to be leaving, but he flew on toward night and his next adventure and if a tear fell across his scales, he never told another soul."

As she finished reading these words aloud, Gustavia looked up at the faces of the children who had been listening to her with rapt attention. It wasn't just her words they found utterly fascinating; this woman was a feast for young eyes. With rings on every finger, strings of beads around her neck sparkling in the light and bells entwined in the complex arrangement of her braids, she jingled and tinkled musically with each movement. But it was the warmth of her gaze that made them feel safe and loved. It was both the woman and her books that drew them to her readings.

She sat in the corner of the small town library looking at a sea of faces, both children and adults filled the space. Quite a turnout for a Thursday afternoon. She hadn't expected so many.

"Did you like the story?" she asked.

"Yes, Miss Gustavia," they chorused.

Gustavia reached behind her for the box of books she brought to these library readings and began passing out copies to each child. As a prolific author of children's books, she made a comfortable enough living but these moments were the true payoff. There was nothing like the feeling of bringing joy to a child, it was something money just couldn't buy.

When all of the children had returned to their seats, Gustavia realized one little girl had not come forward for a book. She still sat in her chair, eyes downcast, red-faced, every line of her body exuding sadness. Recognizing chronic shyness since it was something she'd had to overcome herself, Gustavia decided there was no way this child would leave without a book.

With five minutes left in her allotted hour, she asked the kids if they had any questions, this was her favorite part of the reading. Their questions often provided her with new perspectives and priceless insights into her characters.

"Why was Ember purple? He's a boy dragon and everyone knows boy dragons are green." The first question came from a boy of six whose mobile features had already perfected a look of scorn. Probably a future banker.

"Because, just like people, dragons come in many colors," she smiled as she answered, "and did you know that purple is the color of royalty? Kings once wore purple robes in case you were thinking it's not a manly enough shade for a dragon." The look of scorn softened to one of speculation.

"Why wasn't there a princess in the story, usually if there's dragons there's princesses." The next question came from a little girl wearing a Cinderella tee shirt.

"Because there are more dragons than there are princesses and purple dragons don't care about titles, especially when they are the adventuring type." That seemed to satisfy the child.

The shy little girl lifted her head with a look of longing on her face that told Gustavia she desperately wanted to ask a question.

Instead, biting her lip in frustration, she looked away. The father sat next to the child, face tensed with despair. Intense brown eyes behind a pair of studious wire rimmed glasses turned toward Gustavia, seeming to beg for something even he was unable to define. A brief moment of eye contact showed his pain.

Hunched in her chair, long blond hair caught in a clumsily wrought tail, the little girl stared at the floor, then every so often flicked a glance up at Gustavia with longing in her eyes. She wanted to participate, was aching to ask a question but, instead was so caught up in shyness or fear that every time her shell began to crack a little, some inner struggle pulled her back

The father watched her battle indecision, turn her head away, and this time when his eyes met Gustavia's she tried to communicate her compassion and understanding, judging she had been successful when she saw his shoulders relax the tiniest bit.

"One last question and then it's time to go," she said.

"Is there going to be another story about Ember?"

"Yes, I think there will be another story. Ember likes his adventures and so do I. Now, that's all the time we have for today. Thank you for listening to my story and I hope to see you again soon." Catching the eye of the shy girl's father she mouthed, "Stay" and saw his answering nod.

As everyone else filed out, Gustavia shook hands and accepted kind words from the parents while taking the time to say a fond goodbye to every child. Then she turned to the father and daughter who remained.

Sitting next to the girl, she leaned down to make eye contact and said gently, "I think you had a question. Everyone else is gone, why don't you ask it now?"

The girl looked around and then soberly asked, "Why didn't Ember have a mommy?" Her question revealed there was a great deal more than simply shyness keeping this adorable child from speaking up, there was also a deep, intense sadness lurking in her eyes.

"That's a really good question. When dragons go on adventures it's because they're old enough to be away from their mommies."

"If he goes too far away, won't his mommy get lost? My mommy got lost, I miss her".

Understanding flashed through Gustavia, her heart nearly breaking with sympathy for this little girl and for the father who was struggling to deal with a complex series of emotions. In a peripheral way, she realized that he was attractive. Frog prince attractive, in other words, just her type. Though this wasn't the moment to be thinking about how he looked. He needed help; she could see he was sinking and everything in her yearned to throw him a lifeline if she could.

"I'm very sorry about your mommy, and I'm sure she misses you, too. What is your name, sweetie?"

"Samantha."

"Well, Samantha," already halfway in love with this child, Gustavia took the girl's small hand in her own, looked squarely into those big brown eyes and tried to find the right words. "I know it's very sad that your mommy is gone but it's okay to feel sad as long as you try and feel happy sometimes, too. Mommies, even mommies who are lost, always want their little girls to be happy."

"Would Ember's mommy want him to be happy if she was lost?"

"She would want her son to be happy, even if she knew he would still miss her. Mothers always want the best for their children, even when sad things happen."

"So my mommy would want me to be happy sometimes, too?" Samantha repeated Gustavia's advice.

Gustavia, heartbroken and wanting to provide what comfort she could, squeezed Samantha's hand gently in both of her own, caressing the soft, petal pink skin. "Yes, because she loved you and she wouldn't want you to be sad all the time."

"Okay," Samantha took a deep breath and sat up a little straighter, some of the sadness falling away, "Okay" she repeated, nodding her head with resolve.

Because there didn't seem to be anything more to say and because both she and the girl's father were nearly in tears, Gustavia scribbled something inside the front cover and handed the girl a book before giving her a big hug. As she did, Samantha's father caught her eye and whispered, "Thank you." Reaching out, she gave his arm a quick squeeze. She noticed he, too, was standing a bit straighter.

Watching the pair of them walk out of the library, Gustavia sighed then conjured up a vision of the two bathed in the white, healing, light and protection she believed the universe provide to those who asked for it. Then, turning her attention back to the task at hand, she helped the library staff put the room to rights and gathered her things. Meanwhile, in the back of her mind, a new story was composing itself, a story about Ember and his lost mother.

AT THE exact moment Gustavia's wishing candle had guttered and gone out, signifying the end of the ritual, Finn Kent had been sitting down to breakfast with his daughter. Another silent breakfast. Another day when nine year old Samantha had, so far, remained essentially mute.

Each day, as she became more withdrawn, he, he feared she might stop speaking altogether. It was worse than ever as anniversary of her mother's death approached. He was at his wits end. Yesterday she had spoken only once, in little more than a whisper, to request a particular bed time story.

Sam liked to read. Lila had always said her daughter was born with the bookworm gene.

Right now, she was addicted to a series of books by someone named Miss Gustavia. Her favorites were the ones about the wicked witch raising her poor, innocent granddaughter. There were four books in that series and he knew she had read them over and over. So had he.

Bed time stories were one of their favorite activities. Recently the author had released the first book in a new series about a dragon named Ember and next week Miss Gustavia was scheduled to do a reading at the local library.

Finn had already built the time into his work schedule to take Samantha to the reading. He had a wild idea that this would give her something to look forward to and maybe get her talking again. It was odd to hope that a chance meeting with some stranger in a library might help turn things around but he was desperate.

"Anything on your schedule for next Thursday?" He asked. Sam glanced at him, eyes wide. She'd heard him talking to Grandma about scheduling a meeting with a child psychologist and then done a web search to see what that might mean. It was a doctor who would want to talk with her. Worse, the doctor would want Samantha to do most of the talking.

"Did you hear me, Sam?" She shrugged then shook her head.

"I said: how would you like to meet Miss Gustavia next Thursday?" He watched her carefully, trying to gauge her reaction.

Sam's head lifted and he could see the excitement begin to steal over her as she realized exactly what he had asked.

"Miss Gustavia? Oh, yes please." Five words. Five short words in a row. The most words at one time all week. He was on the right track. Thursday couldn't come soon enough for him but, in the meantime, he planned to build on that foundation of excitement, see if he could get more out of her.

Things were looking up.

CHAPTER TWO

Present Day

"You've already met him, the cards don't lie." Kat tapped a fingernail on the two of cups while Gustavia, usually the picture of patience and good will, rolled her eyes then immediately felt bad even though she knew the psychic couldn't see the gesture.

Kat was blind.

Traumatized as a teenager when her psychic gift allowed her to see spirits, Kat had inexplicably begun to lose her vision. Now, diagnosed with a form of hysterical blindness, she used a tarot deck embossed with braille to give readings.

"I think I would have remembered meeting my soul mate," Gustavia argued with the woman who was one of her closest friends, "and I didn't come here to get a reading about my love life, or my lack of one." Sweeping up the cards laid in a cross pattern on the table, frustration sharpening each motion, she reshuffled them back into the deck, cut the cards and handed them to Kat asking her to lay them out again.

The sign on the front of her door said Madame Zephyr, Psychic Readings but Kathleen Travers, Kat to her friends, was not the stereotypical psychic. Sitting at the table in her sunny, lavender-scented dining room, the twenty something woman, dark hair falling around her face, did not give off an other-worldly vibe.

Gustavia, dressed in a floaty skirt in a stylized floral pattern, chunky sandals showing off a series of toe rings, draped in beaded necklaces and wearing bells woven into her hair did fit the part.

Over the past three months, Gustavia and Kat had become embroiled in an adventure of sorts. It all started when Gustavia brought her best friend Julie in for a reading that had been more than any of them bargained for. Kat had channeled Julie's grandmother, Estelle, and also her great grandfather, Julius, the spirits sending them all on a quest for a cache of hidden family heirlooms. Aura reader, Amethyst, had been drawn into the intrigue and so had journalist turned historian, Tyler Kingsley.

By the time the dust settled, Julie and Tyler were engaged, the family silver had been found, Julie's ex fiancé, who turned out to be a con man, was on the run and they'd learned there were three more caches hidden somewhere in the house.

For Kat, the most surprising development occurred when her vision returned each time she channeled Estelle. This confirmed her doctor's diagnosis of hysterical blindness and gave her hope that somehow, someday, she would see again.

"Tarot always shows what is most needed, rather than what is most wished for," she explained with a mixture of exasperation and humor, since Gustavia's past three readings had centered on her love life no matter what question she had asked. "Are you sure you don't remember meeting someone? You meet a lot of people when you do readings and other promotions, maybe he attended one of them."

"Wouldn't I have seen a rainbow or shooting sparks or at least heard a bell ringing?"

"Gustavia, you wear bells in your hair or around your neck most of the time, so I'm pretty sure you hear them ringing all day long. Besides, don't you know, bells are for when angels get their wings?" Kat answered dryly, "And don't roll your eyes at me again".

Instantly contrite, Gustavia apologized for being frustrated while she wondered how Kat knew about the eye rolling.

"I'm sorry, I don't know what has come over me, lately. I've been feeling unbalanced, unsettled." There was no sense in adding lonely to the list, she wasn't looking for sympathy. Watching Julie and Tyler connect had been lovely. Truly happy for her friend, Gustavia was getting tired of feeling lonely. When would it be her turn?

"Have you seen Amethyst? Maybe your aura needs to be cleared or your chakras are out of alignment."

Gustavia sighed, bracing an elbow on the table; she rested her cheek in her palm and looked at the new card layout. It was eerily similar to the first even after a thorough shuffling.

Lips quirking, Kat ran her sensitive fingers over the raised bumps, dryly pointing out that the new cards, though slightly different, spoke the same message as the first set.

Masterfully suppressing an eye roll in favor of a

curled lip and a near snarl, Gustavia searched for some nuance that neither of them had noticed. She would have liked to argue with Kat but she could see the combination of cards on the table bore out the psychic's interpretation, whether she liked it or not.

It wasn't that Gustavia was rebelling against romance or the notion of already having met her soul mate. It was the five horrible dates she had been on in the past few months, the idea that one of these guys was destined to complete her was daunting to say the least.

"Do you think we could narrow it down a little? I think I'm a positive person but if it's that guy with the violent purple and orange aura, I'm not sure if spending the rest of my life wearing sunglasses is going to work for me. Or, maybe it's the one who called me a weirdo five minutes into the date then spent an hour telling me about how he collects his own toenail clippings. He keeps them in a jar and I'm the weirdo?"

Smothering a smile, Kat replied, "Gustavia, stop. You know your soul mate would have to be someone just as wonderful and giving as you are, or it wouldn't be a perfect match." Kat continued, "Remember you had a reading with almost these exact same cards about a year ago so I'm thinking it may be someone you met then. Someone who didn't become part of your life at the time."

"Phew," Gustavia perked up considerably at the thought, her usual cheerful smile springing back to life. "I hope so because the idea of a long term relationship with any of my most recent dates would make me seriously doubt my ability to create good Karma."

"Speaking of good Karma, my niece just loves your latest book and being able to give her a copy the day before it was released made me a hero."

"My agent wanted me to do an extended book tour; she said it would ramp up sales. Then she politely suggested that I might want to make some changes to my appearance, maybe tone down what she called the unconventional factor," She did the air quotes gesture.

"Are you going to do the tour? Maybe that's where you'll bump into your soul mate again."

"No. I'd have to miss out on the next phase of the treasure hunt. Sales are growing steadily anyway, so I'm planning to stick with the usual promotional venues. There's the library reading here on Thursday then I'll do five or six more in the city over the next few weeks. Maybe he'll be there. Maybe he's only six years old and it's our tragic destiny to be star crossed because of our age difference," Gustavia joked resting the back of her hand on her forehead dramatically, forgetting for a moment that Kat could not see the gesture.

Kat laughed at the thought, but her gifts went beyond reading cards or channeling spirits and she knew Gustavia was in for a bit of a ride. Soul mate or not, the man she saw portrayed in the reading was carrying heavy baggage related to a loss and there were dark clouds on the horizon. Gustavia still had Julie's ex—the madman Logan—to deal with.

But most importantly, before Gustavia could find love, she needed to deal with a long running family rift. That was in the cards also, but during every reading, when Kat brought up the topic, Gustavia shut it back down. Forcefully.

Gustavia might end up alone and hurting if she didn't learn to accept and return the love that was coming her way. All the love, from every source.

Thankfully, there was also the potential for great happiness. Gustavia would need guidance and Kat hoped she was up to the challenge. No matter what happened, she intended to do her best to help.

Kat knew exactly what it felt like to be lonely, it wasn't as though men were lining up to date blind psychics. In fact, most of the men she met were coming to her seeking advice about dealing with a bad relationship or were workaholics looking for help with career advancement. On some level, she felt her work made her unnaturally jaded when it came to romantic relationships.

It was rare to see a reading that included soul mates. It was much more common when people could choose from many paths that might lead to love. Those were the clients she found easiest to help. Look at their options, find the closest path with the fewest obstacles and gently set them on their way, give them a nudge here and a subtle push there and next thing you know—bam, true love.

Soul mates only had one relationship, one path to true love and often it was a rocky one. Sometimes their soul mate had already passed on, or they had missed their opportunity early on in life.

In those cases, she had to make a choice. Find a path that would bring them as close to happiness as possible or acknowledge that she'd never be able to help them find love and hope that they wouldn't become bitter.

Either way, it looked like Gustavia might finally get her chance, with a little guidance. It was a lot of responsibility. Something she did not take lightly.

CHAPTER THREE

"Come on, Samantha. If you don't get moving we're not going to make it to the library in time for the reading."

"Daddy, I need to find that book she signed for me last time, I want to show it to her," his ten year old daughter yelled down. "Could we ask Miss Gustavia to lunch? Would that be okay?"

"Sure," he answered, grabbing the book from the hall table where she had left it, Finn Kent called back up the stairs, "I have it, now get down here."

There was no harm in asking but he assumed the author would be too busy doing—well—whatever it was authors do.

Father and daughter were both looking forward to this particular outing, though for different reasons.

Samantha was excited because she felt a personal connection to this newest book. Last year during the reading, she had asked Miss Gustavia a question, one she was sure had led directly to the story line of the newest Ember book.

More than that, the short conversation had taught Samantha that life must go on, even in the face of painful loss.

Finn just wanted the chance to thank the author for reaching out to give him some much needed support at a time when he had been floundering. He wasn't even sure that Gustavia would remember him or his daughter but that moment of compassion she'd shown Samantha had been a turning point. After his wife's death, Samantha had become shy and withdrawn to the point where she barely spoke anymore, even to him.

Taking her to a library reading by her favorite author had been his last ditch effort to try and pull her out of her shell. What he hadn't counted on was Gustavia's ability to quickly grasp the situation and her generosity in taking the time to speak to Samantha one on one. Somehow, she'd known exactly the right thing to say. A miracle.

He was hoping to get a moment alone with her to express his gratitude.

Arriving at the library barely in time, the pair settled in the last two remaining chairs just as Gustavia began to read. During the previous reading, Finn had been too preoccupied to appreciate the expressiveness, the warmth of her voice, the way she was able to draw in both children and parents with her words. Her twinkling eyes when she looked out over her audience and her way of making each person feel as though she were talking only to them.

What he did remember was the kindness he'd seen in her eyes, the gentle way she'd had with his daughter and the warmth of her empathy. Samantha sat on the edge of her seat, head held high as she avidly took in every word.

After a few moments, Gustavia glanced up and

noticed father and daughter. Smiling delightedly at the change she could see in both of them, she made eye contact with the girl giving her a slight nod of recognition. Samantha beamed in response, settled back in the chair and listened to the rest of the story.

As always, Gustavia ended the reading with a short question and answer period and was not surprised to see Samantha's hand waving excitedly in the air. When it was her turn, she asked, "If Ember was a big enough dragon to go on adventures alone, why did he go searching for a mommy?"

"Because, sometimes everyone needs their mommy, even big dragons," Gustavia answered with a smile.

She fielded two or three more questions before passing out copies of the book, saying goodbye and watching everyone but Samantha and her father file out. Gustavia went to them and sitting next to Samantha said, "I was hoping you would be here today and that you would be feeling less sad."

"Look," Samantha said, "I still have that book you signed for me last time."

"Well, here's another one to add to your collection," she scrawled a short message before handing the book to Samantha. "And I am glad to see you again. You've grown a few inches and your smile is so much brighter."

"Yes," answered the girl, "when you told me that mommy would want me to be happy sometimes, I knew it was true. It made me feel better. I even think she'd be happy if I found a new mommy. It wouldn't be the same, but I thought that if I don't have a mommy, maybe somewhere, there is a mommy who doesn't have a little girl and maybe she could be mine. What do you think?"

"That sounds like a very logical idea," and one that touched Gustavia deeply. She glanced over the girl's head to see what the father thought of this plan. Smiling, he shrugged his shoulders in resignation then held out a hand saying, "My name is Finn Kent; we didn't have a chance to officially meet last year."

Gustavia put her hand in his and was surprised to feel a sizzling pulse of recognition swim through her veins at the contact.

"My name's Gustavia, though you probably already knew that. It's nice to meet you." Very nice, she thought. Then she waited for him to ask, as most people did, about the origin of her name but he didn't take the bait.

Instead, he suggested Samantha go pick out some books to borrow.

Once she was out of earshot, he turned to Gustavia and said, "I don't think you could possibly understand what you did for us last year. When we lost Lila, her mother, Samantha couldn't cope. She was becoming more withdrawn every day. I brought her to your reading because I hoped meeting her favorite author might help her find words again." Finn grabbed Gustavia's hand and gave it a quick squeeze. "You said exactly the right thing to her, it was a major turning point for us."

There was that tingle again, it was delicious. So, his round-rimmed glasses were a tiny bit on the geeky side, his hands were warm and the intensity in his clear, brown eyes drew her in until she couldn't quite concentrate on what he was saying.

He felt something, too. Nothing so tame as a tingle;

he felt, instead, a punch to the gut. Then, a click as something he hadn't known was off kilter fell into place. Boom, there she was, his mind insisted. The feeling scared him and his survival instincts told him to turn and run. Fast. Now.

Instead, he stayed. He inhaled the scent of her, floral but also earthy, she smelled like a garden. Like home.

Pulling her hand slowly from his, Gustavia wrenched her mind back to the conversation not realizing Finn was struggling to do the same. "I am glad I could help, your daughter has a lovely aura, she deserves to be happy."

"Aura?" Finn raised an eyebrow. What was she talking about? What had he missed?

"Yes, aura, you know, we all have them," she beamed. "Although, not everyone can see them at first. Yours is very intense."

Unsure of the proper response, Finn just let the comment pass.

He had to get his head down out of the clouds. Look at this thing logically, look at her logically. This time, survival instincts spoke louder than his heart and he pulled back, ruthlessly tamped down the euphoria rising inside him.

Giving her the once over, he noted she was wearing a long skirt with what appeared to be large rainbow colored petals sewn on in an overlapping spiral and a spangled tank top emblazoned with the words *Fairies rule, Dragons drool* across the front. Nothing wrong with that, he appreciated the whimsy.

So what if she had a tiny string of bells braided into her hair. She was a children's book author for Pete's sake, she needed to appeal to the kids, right?

She probably didn't go around looking like one of those edible flowers from Willy Wonka's garden every day. And what did it mean that he was overwhelmed with the urge to take great big bite?

It meant he was losing his mind, that's what.

Logic. Right. Thinking logically, she seemed nice enough but she looked like ten shades of crazy pants, totally not the right kind of person to be hanging around his daughter.

Not dependable, not someone who would stick around.

A flight risk. He knew it. She'd break his daughter's heart.

A thought whispered through him. Break your heart, you mean.

Realizing she had been speaking during the entire time he had been appraising her outfit and declaring her unsuitable for—whatever—he pulled his attention back just in time to hear her say, "In fact, your aura just flashed a lovely shade of red, what were you thinking just now?" Finn decided that he had better decline giving her a truthful answer and changed the subject just as Samantha rejoined them.

"Sam has requested that we offer to take you out to lunch, are you interested?" It was the last thing he wanted to do given his strong reaction to her, the confusion caused by nothing more than her nearness, but he wouldn't go back on a promise. She sensed his reluctance but not the cause.

"Oh, yes, please Miss Gustavia; it would be so much fun," Sam chimed in, "we could go right now." Gustavia hesitated. "Please?"

Resisting Sam was futile. "That sounds lovely but I

have to pack up my things first. Shall I meet you in half an hour?"

"Daddy, can we take her to Tassone's?" It was Sam's favorite place; the pizza cook always made her a smiley face with the pepperoni and black olives.

Finn raised a questioning eyebrow and Gustavia nodded. "I'll meet you there."

Why not?

"Okay, let's let Miss Gustavia get packed up."

Samantha followed her father out the door, looking over her shoulder the whole way. There was something hungry in her gaze, something that touched Gustavia deeply because it was a feeling she recognized.

The girl needed a woman in her life. She'd felt the same way, essentially growing up motherless herself.

Gustavia started life as Eloise Roman, daughter of Congressman Peter and cardiologist Dr. Janine Roman. The year she turned nine, with no warning or reason given, she'd been sent to live with her grandmother on her father's side. Vivian Roman was a very proper and stern woman. She did not understand or approve of Eloise and her increasingly stringent efforts to restrain her granddaughter's more flamboyant nature had had just the opposite effect.

Every day felt like a punishment. With no explanation given, she was left to assume her parent's hadn't wanted her. An assumption Vivian did everything in her power to foster.

So, Eloise got into trouble. A lot of trouble. The year after she went to live with her grandmother, she cut her hair with a pair of kitchen shears and using a temporary dye, turned it all the colors of the rainbow. The act cost her two months of freedom.

When her grandmother found out that she had pierced her own ears, Vivian decreed each afternoon of the next three months would be spent polishing the same silver tea service.

Finally free, during her first year of college, Eloise set the gears in motion to change her name to Gustavia, cut all ties with her grandmother and used those childhood experiences to pen the first of a very successful series of children's books featuring a mean old witch and her sweet and innocent granddaughter.

When she published her second book, as a tribute to her grandmother, Gustavia got a witch tattoo. On her butt.

Whatever mysterious event caused them to give up their free-spirited daughter, both parents continued to maintain their distance as the years passed. Eventually, the only time she saw them was during awkward holiday visits, each year worse than the last.

Now, it had been two years since either Peter or Janine had seen their daughter. Her choice, not theirs. Gustavia would have shocked to learn that they owned a copy of each of her books.

Their strained family dynamic trickled down to impact the relationship between Gustavia and her brother Zack. Both had been sent to Vivian's but after a few months, he returned home while Gustavia stayed on. It broke her heart, nearly broke her spirit and damaged her once close relationship with her younger brother.

Now, thrown together more often, Gustavia understood she couldn't continue to blame him for the past. The siblings were now able to be in the same room for extended periods of time without bickering, it was refreshing.

Still, wary of another rejection, Gustavia held some part of herself in reserve. Trusting him with her life was one thing, he was a cop, it was his duty to protect and serve. Trusting him with the love most families took for granted was another. Keeping her guard up, she thought, was just good common sense.

Chapter Four

Instead of the half hour she'd requested, it only took Gustavia ten minutes to finish up at the library so she was already seated at one of the checkered cloth-covered tables at Tassone's when Finn and Sam arrived. No bad thing since it gave her the chance to watch him walk toward her.

He moved with the loose-hipped grace of someone totally comfortable in his skin, almost a swagger. Snug jeans hugged well-muscled thighs, suggesting the view of him walking away would also be worth an ogle or two. Maybe three. Wide shoulders stretched the simple blue t-shirt, pulling it across a nicely defined chest. But it was his face that threatened to draw purring noises from her lips; warm brown eyes under a wide forehead softened by a lock of hair that she wanted to run her fingers through, slightly square jaw and a set of full, kissable lips made for an amazing total package. He wore a pair of wire rimmed glasses that might have seemed nerdy on anyone else, but on him, the effect was pretty hot. He'd gone from the sad and overwhelmed father she'd seen at her reading a year ago, to this confident, sexy vision. Yum.

Samantha bounced along beside him, blond hair flying as she spotted Gustavia and pulled her father toward the table, her smile lit up the entire restaurant.

Gustavia stood and without thinking twice, pulled the girl into a hug; Sam clung to her with surprising strength while Finn watched them both. Sam needed a woman in her life, he did the best he could, but he was kidding himself if he thought that just having a dad was enough.

Until this minute, the question of whether he was ready to put himself out there and start dating again after losing Lily had not entered his mind.

He became increasingly uncomfortable watching them together; Sam chattered away to this woman as though they'd known each other forever. What a difference a year had made. Emotions welled up and threatened to overwhelm.

Finn had been completely out of his depth when he'd brought Sam to that first reading. His folks had stayed in town to help for as long as they could but eventually he'd been left alone with his daughter, a time consuming business to run and his grief.

He had done the best he could but it hadn't been enough.

Sam looked so much like Lily, it was uncanny but when it came to brooding, she took after him. It was the trait he least liked about himself and the one he found most difficult to change.

As the months passed and she continued to withdraw, he'd tried everything he could think of to pull his daughter back. During those dark months, she'd read and reread every book Gustavia had ever written, the stories and characters bringing her a much needed sense of solace. Finally, when he'd seen the poster in the library saying the author would be giving a reading, some small voice inside him said, "This is it," so he listened and scheduled in the time to attend.

Walking into the library that day had felt like moving through a wall of water that sucked and pulled at him. In a million years, he could never have prepared himself for the way Gustavia had intuitively picked up on Sam's struggle and with a few simple words, begun the process that drained it all away.

It had been life-changing and he owed her a debt. The owing felt heavy on his shoulders.

Lost in remembering, he didn't notice the sudden silence until he realized his tablemates were looking at him expectantly, both sets of eyes twinkling. When they exchanged identical looks of exasperation then started laughing, he knew his inattention had been noticed.

Time to shrug it off.

Smiling, he held up both hands in surrender, "You caught me, I wasn't paying attention, sorry."

"Samantha was just telling me about her room, she says you built her the most amazing bed. Is that what you do for a living? Build beds?"

"I mostly do architectural restoration and general contracting but when I get the chance, I like to build other things. Cabinets, beds, whatever."

"Oh, serendipity."

He quirked an eyebrow.

"I may have a job for you. My friend Julie needs some work done on her house. She's looking for someone to handle the roof work, but, I'll warn you, it's a big job. There's a bunch of peaks and valleys, some steep pitches plus two sections of flat roof, and I know it might not classify as a restoration project but it's a really cool house. "

Now his eyes widened in surprise and it was her turn to smirk.

"Yeah, I know what peaks and valleys are; I've worked with Habitat for Humanity on a few projects. I like building things, using power tools."

Surprise caused him to blunder and say the first thing that came to mind.

"Ah, did you dress like that on the building site? I can't imagine how effective you'd be flouncing around in that kind of get up." He hadn't meant to sound quite so snarky. The words just came out that way.

For a moment, she was speechless; all she could do was look at him incredulously. Then annoyance set in.

Finn watched the play of emotions across her face and knew he'd put his foot in it.

Gustavia had been nothing but nice to both he and his daughter and this was a lousy way to repay her. He didn't know how it happened, hadn't meant to offend, but something about her flipped his switch, turned him surly. He was over it now, but the damage, it seemed, was done.

"Of course I dressed appropriately, I'm not an idiot." Bristling with indignation, she sat back in her chair, folded her arms and pierced him with a steely stare. "Underestimating me rarely ends well; you should keep that in mind."

"Sorry." He sounded sincere but there was still something around the eyes, a lingering bit of mutiny. She was unimpressed. Casting her mind back over the conversation, she couldn't pick up on anything she'd said that might trigger such a reaction so concluded the problem was entirely on him.

This Jekyll and Hyde act could get old in a hurry.

She shook it off and continued, "It's Hayward House, that..."

"I know the one," he interrupted her. "Part Greek, part Gothic with the stained glass windows, right?"

"That's the one. Julie, the owner, is planning some repairs. The roof to start, then new windows. After that, some sprucing and trim work, maybe a few other small changes. Depends on—well, let's just say it depends." She refused to acknowledge his questioning look. "Luckily the foundation is rock solid as are all the supporting joists." Gustavia was beginning to have second thoughts about asking him to bid on the job. This guy gave off a very mixed vibe, his tone earlier was a real turn off.

"Daddy, you should do it, help Miss Gustavia's friend fix up her house. It's what you're best at." This was one job site she would look forward to visiting.

"I'd love to come out and take a look at the job if you could arrange it, I've always wanted to get my hands on that house."

She had reservations, but she'd give him the benefit of the doubt, his attitude might have been a momentary lapse. She hoped so. "I'm sitting for Julie in the studio on Tuesday afternoon. Can you come by then and I'll introduce you?"

"Sure, is 2 o'clock okay?"

"Fine."

And the arrangements were made.

Samantha looked back and forth at the two adults, a grin lighting her face; if her dad got the job, she just knew there would be plenty of chances to visit and hang out with Miss Gustavia again. That would be the coolest thing ever.

"Do you have any kids, Miss Gustavia? How do you come up with ideas for books? Did you write about Ember and his mommy because I asked you that question last year?" Questions came in rapid fire.

"Sam, take a breath and give the woman a chance to speak." Finn cut in before his daughter could ask anything else. Her curious nature was a delight to him but could be a bit much to take.

"I don't have any children, yet. I get my ideas from many places and yes, the story about Ember's mommy was inspired by your question last year." Gustavia smiled as she answered.

"That's so cool, wait until I tell my friends." Sam bounced in her chair.

"Can I ask another question?" She didn't wait for an affirmation. "Did your parents name you Gustavia? Or is it a pen name? It's very unusual. I learned about pen names on the Internet. I like to research things."

Clearly, Gustavia thought in amusement. "No, my parents named me Eloise after my great grandmother. But it just didn't feel like the right name for me so I changed it to something that did."

"How did they react? Your parents." Finn was genuinely curious.

"Not well, but that's a story for another day. I chose it because I thought it would be completely unique."

He thought she was right in that assessment.

Officially known as a pizza joint, Tassone's had a lot more on their menu so Gustavia ordered the eggplant lasagna, while Finn and Sam split a pepperoni and black olive pie. The atmosphere was bright and friendly with outdoor, bistro style seating and a few booths.

Owned by a jolly middle-aged couple who served recipes passed down through the generations, it was a comfortable, family oriented eatery.

For the kids, the owners had installed several vintage video games in the corner. Sam was addicted to Galaga so Finn gave her a quarter and sent her off to play, giving him a chance to speak to Gustavia in private.

He surprised her by saying, "I can't thank you enough for what you did for Sam at your reading last year. You said exactly what she needed to hear and it's made all the difference in the world."

"She's a beautiful girl; you're doing a great job with her." Even though she had reservations about the way he'd spoken to her earlier, Gustavia could tell he was a devoted father. Could be he'd just had an off moment. Just too bad he managed to find her Achilles heel, she'd taken some flack over the years, mostly from her own family, for being a non-conformist.

"It has been a struggle and I'm doing the best I can but she misses her mother. It's been tough on her. By the time we came to your reading last year, she was so withdrawn she barely spoke. She was having trouble in school and I didn't know what more to do." He shook his head as though to fling away the bad memories.

"She refused to talk to a counselor and your books were the only things she was excited about, so when I saw the flier saying you would be at the library, I took a chance that meeting you might—I don't know—give her something more positive to focus on. When you noticed her and took the time to talk to her the way you did—Well, I'm sure it seemed a simple thing to you and easily forgotten, but to her, it was a Rockstar moment.

There are no words to tell you how grateful I am."

Grateful didn't seem the appropriate word given his earlier attitude. Probably she was just blowing the whole thing up in her head.

"How did you know what to say?" He asked.

"Let's just say I understood her feelings and leave it at that." She smiled to soften the mind-your-own-business message.

Gustavia's heart melted when she saw the earnestness in his eyes and she reached out to where his hand rested on the table, covered it with her own, and gave it a squeeze. "I'm glad to have helped, but I think you should give yourself the credit, you stayed proactive, paid enough attention to her interests to know what might help. In my book, that makes you Superdad. You even have the right last name for the title." She grinned at him than waggled her eyebrows to lighten the mood. "You're probably wearing the costume under those clothes right now."

That thought led her down the path of wondering just what might be lurking under his t-shirt and jeans, but she pulled her thoughts back before she said or did something to embarrass herself. There were times when her internal filters weren't strong enough to keep her from speaking her thoughts aloud. Got her into trouble now and then. She hoped he couldn't read her mind, that would be bad, very bad.

That tingle again. Despite how nice it felt, he snatched his hand back as though he'd just realized he was touching a snake. Gustavia's eyes widened in surprise then narrowed.

What was his deal?

He returned her gaze with a level stare of his own.

Fine. If that's how he wanted it.

Finn was conflicted, Gustavia had helped him, helped his daughter, but he didn't want them getting too involved. The last thing Sam needed was another female role model who might eventually leave. There was no way he wanted to see her go down that particular rabbit hole again.

Then, there was the attraction he was beginning to feel. It complicated things. Okay, he wanted her. He just didn't want to want her.

Still, he was appalled at himself for the way he'd spoken to this woman after she'd been so unfailingly kind. Some gratitude he'd shown. What was wrong with him? And who names their kid Gustavia, anyway?

His thoughts were on a seesaw.

It was like one of those dreams where you knew something was going to happen but felt paralyzed, unable to stop it. She had a light in her and such gentleness and yet with every passing moment, the need to push her away grew within him. And that would have been fine if the need to get closer to her hadn't been growing just as strong. She was warm and funny and quirky and genuine. Confident but not arrogant. Everything he admired in a woman. Everything he wanted to avoid.

Samantha and the food arrived at the table at the same time; Gustavia, knowing a bit more about the family history, now listened to her chatter with a different ear. Underneath the questions, she heard the loneliness that a girl with no mother inevitably felt. Everything in her yearned to try and fill that void. Too bad her father was so prickly, it would be hard to get close to the one without having to deal with the other.

She sighed.

Finn subsided into a brooding silence while Gustavia and Samantha talked. He noted that the woman did not talk down to the child, that she was considerate and engaged with his daughter. Eventually, his mood darkened the atmosphere to the point that even Sam was looking at him questioningly so he abruptly announced, "We should be going now," and reached for his wallet.

Great, Gustavia thought, something really has crawled up his backside and I practically begged him to submit a quote for Julie. Just my luck, she'll probably accept. She wasn't looking forward to dealing with someone who ran hot then cold more rapidly than the shower in a cheap motel.

In her experience, people who judge based on her clothing choices tended to jump to conclusions about her. Unflattering conclusions. That she was some kind of flighty, new age, crazy chick. She'd admit to playing into those impressions at times and it hadn't taken years of psychoanalysis for her to understand she used her appearance as a weapon against her family.

By now, Finn was also regretting his decision to make a bid for the Hayward House job. If it meant spending more time with Gustavia, he'd probably be better off walking away. She unsettled him. Still, it wasn't every day he got the chance to add a job like this to his resume.

Better keep the appointment, and so deciding, he made the effort to at least be cordial even if the damage was already done. There was no way, he thought, that she would ever forgive his erratic behavior.

With Sam practically dancing between them, the pair strolled down the street toward the parking lot, both lost in their thoughts.

The minute they rounded the corner, Finn knew exactly which car belonged to Gustavia and, sure enough, she made a beeline for the rust-colored but mint condition, vintage Ford Maverick. Pulling a huge wad of keys from her voluminous straw bag, she reached down to unlock the door as he took a turn around the car, whistling softly, incredulously.

The exterior was pristine but she'd worked her magic on the inside.

She'd replaced the headliner with her own hand-crafted version made from fabric in a moon and stars pattern, then pinned on a grid of wire-wrapped crystals. The vinyl seats were covered in a re-purposed, rainbow-dyed chenille bedspread. For the final touch, she'd used gold paint on every body-colored metal interior area, decorating with designs ranging from Celtic to Japanese calligraphy. The patterns contained charms against everything from accidents to traffic tickets. On the dashboard lived her protective angel, an old grass-skirted hula dancing doll who'd been refitted with a gypsy outfit and a pair of angel wings.

Before he could help himself, Finn threw his head back and laughed in appreciation. It was spectacular. Unique, just like her.

A work of art. He loved it.

Gustavia wrongly interpreted his response, coming as it did on the heels of his comment about her clothing. She assumed the worst.

He was laughing at her baby.

With a terse, "See you Tuesday." She quickly slid into the seat, started car with a vicious twist of her wrist and while he watched in surprise, drove away without even saying goodbye to Samantha. How rude.

CHAPTER FIVE

Speeding down the road, Gustavia cranked up the stereo to blasting and loosed a series of words fit to burn the ears off a sailor. Her upright, uptight grandmother would have been thoroughly appalled. Picturing the pinched look her words would have put on Vivian's face was satisfying but still better to cut of thoughts of the woman. Those never led to anything good.

Before she'd even made the conscious decision to go there, she found herself turning down the drive to Hayward House. She needed to rant, she needed her best friend. She needed Julie.

Normally she slowed and enjoyed the spectacular view as she turned the corner leading to the house, but today Gustavia barely noticed its unique architecture.

Classic Greek revival style columns marched across the centrally located entrance below an elongated, triangle-shaped pediment. It was the smaller wings on either side where the design went a bit wonky. In order to install four stained glass windows, two in front and two in back, Julie's great grandfather had raised the roof line to add towering Gothic spires complete with elaborately scrolled trim.

The clean, white, straight and graceful lines of the Greek should have been totally at odds with the gingerbread color and feel of the Gothic. Yet, somehow, it all worked together. Warm, welcoming and totally quirky, the house had always appealed to Gustavia's unique artistic sensibilities.

She loved the house; it was the first place where everyone had ever loved her unconditionally. Julie and her grandmother Estelle treated her like family. It felt like home.

Because this was her home too, she had been thrilled to help when a ghostly encounter this past spring had sparked a full on treasure hunt. What was supposed to be a simple Tarot card reading had turned into a ghostly encounter that provided a cryptic set of clues that she, Julie and a group of friends had navigated to locate a cache of family heirlooms that Julie's great grandfather had hidden in the library.

Over the three month period of their search, her best friend had found love and enough of her lost family fortune to begin some much needed repairs. The repairs, for which she, Gustavia, had just, without even asking Julie first, invited that odious man to submit an estimate.

Propelled by outrage, she wrenched open the large front door, entered the alarm code and called out, "Hey Jules, where are you?"

"Studio," Came the distant reply.

Julie, a talented photographer, was seated at her computer working on a series of images from a fashion shoot she'd done earlier in the week. Glancing up, it only took one look at Gustavia's face to see something had happened so Julie saved her work then led her friend to the kitchen to make a pot of calming herbal tea. It was their go-to stress reliever.

"All right, who peed in your cornflakes? Someone in your family call?" Family encounters always sent Gustavia into a tailspin.

"No but it might as well have been my family, it felt the same to me."

"Wait a minute, wasn't your reading at the library on for today?"

"Yes and that little girl came back. The sad one from last year, you remember? The one who lost her mom and I wrote the new Ember because of her. Well, she and her dad took me to lunch." She practically sneered the word.

"Sounds like a nice thing for them to do. So, how did it go wrong? I assume it went wrong."

Unable to settle, Gustavia paced the floor in a fit of pique, skirts swirling as her long legs flashed underneath, tinkling sounds from various adornments punctuated her mutters.

Stalking over to the table, she leaned down and placed both hands on the edge of its polished surface, eyes sparking as she spit out the words.

"I don't know what's wrong with that man. I don't flounce around, do I? Do I? Flounce. What kind of word is that?" Restless, she pushed away from the table to pace the length of the room again.

"He said you flounced? In what context? While you were reading to the kids?" It was a rare thing to see Gustavia so worked up about a man. He must have made quite an impression. Julie's lips wanted to quirk into a smile but she wisely relaxed her face.

"No, we were talking about my Habitat projects and about him maybe doing some roof work here and then he questioned my abilities. Asked me something about whether or not I flounce around on a job site dressed like this."

Julie knew the comment was the equivalent of an atomic bomb and the poor guy probably had no idea the depth of his insult. Gustavia gloried in being different, being herself no matter the cost. However, she took a dim view of anyone who picked on others for the way they dressed or for their beliefs.

Whenever she observed that type of judgmental behavior, she took up the banner and marched into the crusades. Still, she wasn't the type to belabor a point, generally being content to have her say then move on. One of her finest qualities was that outside of her family, Gustavia never held a grudge.

"First he's all humble, thanking me for helping to pull his daughter out of her shell, then the next minute he assumes I'm some kind of empty-headed, rainbow-loving, new age bimbo who dresses inappropriately and couldn't possibly know the handle from the business end of a hammer."

Gustavia was still ranting when Julie's fiancé, Tyler walked into the room. He'd been practicing his ability to see auras and after taking one look at Gustavia's, announced that hers had gone a funny set of colors and was pulsing. Julie took great delight in suggesting a trip to see Amethyst, their good friend the aura specialist. She felt it was poetic justice after having been dragged, against her wishes, to see the woman several times recently.

Her suggestion was met with a derisive sniff that

made her giggle. Her giggle was met by another sniff accompanied by a raised eyebrow which only made it worse and pretty soon Julie was holding her aching stomach and wiping tears from her eyes as Gustavia stood silently glaring, wholly unamused.

"Oh, come on. You know I'm not laughing at you."

"At me, about me. Same thing."

"Sorry," Julie meant the words. "Really. I am sorry. It's just the thought of hauling you off to Amethyst's got me going."

Still amused but understanding that her friend was genuinely upset, Julie wrapped an arm around Gustavia's waist and led her to the table, settled her in a chair and poured fresh tea. Clearly this guy had made an impression and not a favorable one.

"And, the worst of it is he's coming here on Tuesday to take a look at the roof."

Now it was Julie's turn to raise an eyebrow. Not because Gustavia had taken it upon herself to request an estimate, the two women were more like sisters than friends so it would have felt natural for Gustavia to step in when she saw an opportunity to help. But, if he had been that rude and was still invited to bid on the job, there must be something more to the situation.

Gustavia sighed, "His daughter is so sweet. It breaks my heart to see what she's been through. He's so gentle with her and you couldn't help but see the love radiating in his aura whenever he looked at her. Guy like that can't be all bad, right?"

"Probably not." And there was the Gustavia she knew so well. The woman who always looked for the best in people unless they gave her no other choice. Julie's crazy ex had been just such a person. A con man and a thief, Gustavia had him pegged from day one. Now, he was on the run and if he had an ounce of common sense, he'd stay that way.

"And he's easy on the eyes. Sort of nerd meets construction worker."

Aha—Julie thought. There it is. She's attracted to him.

"Perfect eyebrows, not too bushy but not thin either and very expressive. They looked soft." Gustavia had a thing for eyebrows.

"So, he's an attractive man and a good father whose major offense was underestimating your construction experience?"

When you put it that way, Gustavia thought, it didn't sound quite so bad.

But she wasn't ready to let him fully off the hook.

"He laughed at my car." Gustavia squeezed a few drops of agave nectar into her cup stirring viciously, she wasn't quite ready to let go of the annoyance. It felt too good.

Undeniably, he got her blood boiling in more ways than one.

"SAMANTHA," Finn called up the stairs. "Come help me with dinner. Set the table, then you can tear up some romaine for the salad."

"Can I add some dried cranberries, too? And maybe some walnuts?"

They worked well together and she was learning how to cook.

Sam loved tearing romaine, the crisp leaves made yummy crunching noises as she pulled them from the tougher stems. It smelled so fresh and green, just like it tasted. While her fingers continued to complete the task, her mind was focused on a question she wanted to ask.

"Daddy, did Miss Gustavia do something wrong? Are you mad at her?"

"No, of course not. Why? Did she say something?" He cursed his wandering attention.

"No. She didn't say anything but you had that somebody-is-in-trouble look on your face." She anxiously waited for him to clarify the situation. Miss Gustavia was the nicest, sweetest person and Sam was hoping to see her more often.

Finn was torn. He really liked Gustavia; she was a breath of air and light in a sometimes stale and pallid world. Just too bad his reaction to her turned his knees to jelly. In both good and bad ways. Clearly, though, his mixed feelings about the woman showed and his daughter, who took after her mother in that respect, was perceptive enough to see them.

"Ah, Sam, it's complicated."

"Dad," she replied in exasperation, "being mad is like a yes or no question." Being young, she would see it that way. It was easier to let her assume it was simply annoyance he felt for Gustavia rather than the possibility of a bone-deep connection that led to sheer terror.

Worse, he knew Gustavia wasn't entirely ambivalent toward him either. A man knew when a woman was admiring his butt. Five minutes of talking to her told him he really had nothing to fear from her, at least on Sam's account. If Gustavia came into his daughter's life, she would be there, rock solid. Why did that scare him?

And wouldn't that make things worse all around if he decided to pursue a relationship with her and it didn't work out? Better for both of them to keep her at arm's length. Safer that way.

Safer for him if he didn't have to see that smile every day, to imagine sucking those rings from her toes, one at a time. He tamped that image down as quickly as it rose to the surface and tried not to imagine how she would taste, how the texture of her skin would feel against his own.

While these thoughts spun through his head, his daughter watched him, trying to gauge his intentions.

CHAPTER SIX

On Tuesday afternoon, even though Gustavia arrived early at Hayward house, Finn's truck was already parked in the drive and he was leaning against the fender. Before she could help herself, the sight of him drew an appreciative hum from her lips. One that with an effort, she turned to a snarl.

The man made her feel all prickly and defensive. She was tempted to walk right past him. Or to flounce. Since stomping past him angrily would fit the true definition of the word.

Hoping she'd forgotten his bad behavior at lunch, Finn came around and opened the door for her saying, "Thanks for allowing me the chance to take a look at the place; it really is a masterpiece of alternative architecture."

Giving her the once over, he was pretty sure she had at least twenty pewter charms hanging from the lattice-like hairstyle she'd created with a series of thin tails, sectioned and secured with tiny, multi-colored rubber bands. A closer look revealed that each charm was in the shape of an angel. She wore a skirt that appeared to have been hand crafted from recycled men's ties and silk scarves. It was certainly a one of a kind item of clothing.

Complimenting her on the outfit seemed like a bad idea so he did it anyway. He admired art in all its forms. Come to think of it, he flat admired her form.

"Nice outfit, very inventive." What he'd said was something he considered a high compliment, what she heard was him calling her a whack-a-doodle.

Let it go, she told herself as every cell in her body urged her to throw down.

Instead, she whirled and opened the trunk to pull out the bag of clothing Julie had asked her to bring for the shoot, an art series following up on her well-received blue woman images which also featured Gustavia.

Finn reached for the bag at the same time. Least he could do was carry her things. Be gentlemanly. He wasn't prepared when she tried to yank the bag from him. A short struggle ensued before he finally let go, lifting both hands and shrugging to show he had given in.

Now, Gustavia was more tempted than ever to flounce but instead, she just stood waiting for him to make the next move.

When he did, it was unexpected. As though nothing had happened, he gestured toward the house and said, "Interesting architectural choices."

Well, if he could act like everything was normal, so could she. Still, there was a distinct coolness to her tone. Practically arctic.

He wasn't oblivious to her reaction, just couldn't seem to find his footing around her. The best thing would be to strike a balance between being friendly and keeping enough distance that his attraction to her would no longer be a factor. So far, that plan was an epic failure.

"I know. Julie's grandfather was somewhat eccentric. He made a lot of changes in order to add those gorgeous stained glass windows.

"They really don't go with the rest of the house," he observed mildly, trying not to get pulled around by the undercurrents he suddenly sensed in the conversation.

"I know. He had his reasons." Gustavia saw no need to elaborate on those reasons to someone who was little more than a total stranger. "Want to meet the owner, take a look inside or is just seeing the outside enough?"

"I want to see it all if I can. Do you know if she's gotten any estimates on the work yet?"

"A few last year, but not since—well, not lately, that's on her to do list. So you can be the first if you're still interested." Gustavia could see that he was, that the architecture created by combining two very different building styles intrigued him. If she hadn't seen the obvious approval and admiration in his eyes, she would have booted him off the property in a hot minute.

Gustavia knocked then opened the door, calling out to Julie and didn't get two steps inside before Lola came barreling at her, then stopped and did what everyone had dubbed "the Lola dance".

Finn laughed at the dog, "Does she think she's a Chihuahua or something?" Lola twisted her body into a c-shape and bounced with all four feet off the ground. Then, for step two in the dance, she reared up on her hind legs with a big doggy grin on her face and pounced with her front feet. Pure joy radiated from the big boxer.

Lola noticed Finn, she stopped and appraised him;

he stood quietly under her gaze. After a moment, she decided he was okay and began to dance again, this time for his benefit.

Unable to resist, Gustavia sank to the floor to give the tawny dog a cuddle while Finn watched, grinning. They made a nice tableau, Julie thought as she entered the room. The unconventionally handsome man watching Gustavia as she talked baby talk to Lola lying in her lap.

After giving the dog one last rub behind the ears, Gustavia stood and introduced Finn to her best friend. "He'd like the tour if you have time, or I can take him around the house." She ignored Julie's subtly questioning look and tried to convey telepathically her intention to just let things play out. A slight shrug told her that Julie had gotten the idea.

"You know the place as well as I do, does he know about the..."

"No, not yet."

Finn frowned. There it was again, they were keeping something from him. He waited patiently for an explanation but it seemed none was forthcoming. "I've been here before. Not inside the house, but when I was younger, my mother brought me to the museum," he told Julie.

"Really? When and what did you think of it?" She was curious since so few people ever attended it had seemed like a waste of her grandmother's time.

Finn felt as though he were being measured and his response was important. "Fifteen years or so ago. I thought Julius Hayward was a visionary. Way ahead of his time. You know, some of those inventions were not that far off the mark and with some updates, could be more viable today than when he invented them."

He could tell he'd surprised both women based on the two sets of raised eyebrows they presented him with. "You mean to tell me no one has ever come around with an offer to buy his plans? Must be worth a fortune to the right person. Someone with a like mind."

"No, that's never happened, and since his notes and plans are missing, it's probably a moot point, anyway." It had never occurred to Julie that the inventions might have any monetary value, or that his work might still be useful. Julius, she was sure, would be proud to extend his legacy.

Meanwhile, she cast an assessing eye over Finn and Gustavia, then decided to let her friend do the honors of providing the tour and with a wicked gleam in her eye, excused herself claiming she had work in her studio. Maybe a bit more time in each other's company would smooth out the rough edges.

Finn's interest in the house had nothing to do with family legends, hidden wealth or Estelle's moderately famous art. For him, the attraction was all about its bones, its structure; he was entranced by the carved moldings and mantels, the coffered and tray ceilings, the craftsmanship of the cabinetry in the library and, of course, the stained glass windows.

When he saw the words solstice and equinox carved into the frames, he asked if Gustavia knew their history. She tried to shrug his questions off casually, but she was pretty sure he'd picked up that she was holding back some vital piece of information.

Once he had seen the inside, he went back to his truck and grabbed a ladder off the rack. "It's okay if I go up today and take a look, right? Take some measurements."

"Sure, let me throw on a pair of jeans and I'll go up and show you what we've done in the way of temporary repairs." It still surprised him that she knew anything about carpentry. "I won't be five minutes," and she went into the house where she always kept a few things. A holdover from her time here between college and buying her own place.

Yelling to Julie that she was taking him up to the roof, Gustavia ran up the stairs and quickly changed before meeting Finn at the bottom of the ladder. He gestured for her to go first so she did, allowing him to enjoy the view of her well-shaped backside as it swayed up the ladder above him.

If she was hoping for an apology or even an acknowledgment that he'd been rude at their last meeting, Gustavia was going to be disappointed. She realized this as the day wore on and they talked of nothing but the structure. With its complicated mixture of architectural styles, there was the area of hipped roof in the center, then two small sections of flat roof connecting to several steep gables where the Gothic turrets had been added. It was a complicated mess not only because of the different roofing styles but also because of the range of materials used.

Scrambling over every section and taking measurements, he could see that the patching they'd done was competent and that he'd probably made a mistake in his estimation of Gustavia's abilities. Still he didn't apologize. It was probably better if he let her keep thinking he was an insensitive jerk.

Simpler that way. Safer.

He told himself the smart choice was to walk away

now, not submit an estimate and be done with the whole thing. With her.

Instead, he finished taking measurements and started a materials list.

Julie watched appraisingly as the two of them climbed back down the ladder. Knowing Finn for all of an hour, his body language told her exactly nothing; Gustavia's, however, was extremely eloquent. The set of her shoulders and the stiffness of her posture were good indicators of her annoyance level.

Stifling a smile, Julie also observed several sidelong glances from each of them and a little extra something in Gustavia's walk. Conclusion? Gustavia might be annoyed but she was also attracted. So was he.

The two women, by unspoken mutual agreement, watched Finn, arm muscles bunching, carry the ladder across the lawn and hoist it back onto the rack on his truck. When Gustavia heard Julie give a sigh of approval, she speared her with a narrow-eyed mock glare and teased. "Hey, what would Tyler say if he saw you gawking at another guy?"

"Oh, I can look, the real question is: are you gonna touch? You know you want to, I can tell."

"After the other day? The way he talked to me?" Gustavia's voice rose.

"He seems to have gotten over that. Maybe he was just having an off day."

Gustavia grumbled, "More like an off life. Today he called my clothes inventive." She didn't mention the tussle over the bag.

"Could have been a compliment." Julie commented,

looking to add a positive spin and getting a dirty look in response.

"He has a daughter. She's great but that makes it complicated."

"You love kids, I can't see that being a problem for you, unless it's a problem for him. Did he give you the vibe? Before things went south, I mean."

"I'm not sure. At first, he was really sweet and thanked me for helping his daughter." She told Julie about Lila and Sam's reaction to losing her. "Then he told me how my conversation with her had been a turning point, he called it a miracle. I'm already half in love with Sam, more than half. She has a bright aura, so light. She's articulate and engaged."

Julie nodded.

"But then he went all weasel on me."

Finn walked around the truck as he secured the ladder and now it was Gustavia's turn to sigh in appreciation. "He's easy on the eyes, no question. He thinks I'm weird, though. I can tell, he thinks I'm ten shades of crazy pants. He's moody and he laughed at my car. Then, today he says my clothes are inventive and acts like everything is just peachy. I can't keep up with the changes."

"You do have an effect on people." Julie smiled; she knew being uncompromisingly true to herself had cost Gustavia over the years. "But if he asks, you're going to see him again? Does he get the benefit of the doubt?"

"Well, I'm not totally stupid; did you get a look at him walking away?" The only answer she got was the waggle of Julie's eyebrows. "Sure is a nice view."

She sighed. "Nice butt even if sometimes it's on his shoulders—not much of a draw. Still, there are flashes of sweet and funny and warm. Might balance out. He's not interested, anyway."

Julie disagreed but kept her thoughts to herself.

The two women strolled toward the truck; it was time to see what Finn thought of the roof. "How long will it take you to get an estimate together?"

"Give me a couple of days to sketch out a materials list and scope of work sheet." He bit the bullet and said, "You did a good job nursing it along."

"Listen, we're having a cookout on Saturday afternoon, why don't you join us. Bring your estimate." Julie wasn't above some subtle matchmaking even when it netted her a sharp elbow jab to the ribs.

"Okay if I bring my little girl with me? Is Lola good with kids?"

"Of course you can. Lola's good with everyone who isn't my crazy ex, but that's a story for another day." The women exchanged a grin though under the levity Finn sensed they'd been through something serious together, but he refrained from asking questions about things that weren't really any of his business.

CHAPTER SEVEN

"It's Saturday, I get to see Miss Gustavia again. I've been counting down the days on my calendar."

"You'll be seeing Miss Gustavia, and her friend Julie who owns the house. Be on your best behavior, don't ask a million questions and did I tell you Julie has a dog? Her name is Lola and she's very friendly but she's also big so you need to be careful around her, okay?"

He glanced at his daughter as she wiggled excitedly beside him in the truck's seat, trying to get a good look out the window to see if they were getting close.

"I will, daddy, I promise, and I won't pester Miss Gustavia or her friends. What do you think they're like? Do you think they're all writers, too? Do you think there'll be burgers? Or maybe hot dogs? I love hot dogs. With relish. Do you think they'll have relish? Oh, and honey mustard, that's my all-time favorite." Finn couldn't help the smile that stole across his face; it never failed to lift his heart when he saw her excited about anything after those scary months of near silence.

He'd even tolerated a gaggle of girls for a birthday sleepover and if they'd made him an honorary princess complete with painted nails and a pink crown, no one ever had to know. There weren't pictures to prove it, at least not any that would ever see the light of day.

Finally, they rounded the corner and the big house came into view, it was impressive enough to pull a soft exclamation out of Sam.

"It's really something isn't it? See those columns? They were part of the original Greek revival style, look at the cornices. The frieze and architrave need a bit of a spruce but everything is solid. It looks like he altered both wings so he could add those Gothic buttresses on either side. Then the stained glass windows—they're just amazing. There are two more on the back side of the house."

Now, it was his daughter's turn to be amused as he pointed out more parts of the architecture and how the styles had been melded. She didn't care about all the fancy words he was throwing around, this house looked a lot like a castle and that was good enough for her.

Catching sight of Gustavia retrieving a cooler from the back seat of her vintage Maverick, Sam pushed the truck door open and jumped out almost before her father could bring it to a full stop. Shrugging off his sharp reprimand, she made a beeline for Gustavia and bounced in place while asking, "Can I help you carry something?"

"Sure," Finn caught Gustavia's eye over his daughter's head, "But I think your father was telling you how dangerous it can be to open the door on a moving car." She cautioned.

"I'm sorry, Dad, I'll be more careful next time." Sam shuffled her feet in chagrin; she didn't want him to be angry with her any more than she wanted Miss Gustavia to think she was a rule-breaker.

Satisfied with that, Finn greeted Gustavia. She wasn't dressed quite as flamboyantly today as she had been before, but he figured it was a safe bet her wardrobe was always going to lean toward the esoteric. Well, that was fine by him, he liked the way she looked, it fit her warm, earth mother personality. He liked that she didn't blend in.

Oh, who was he kidding, she'd draw the eye of everyone in any room she entered and her clothing choices were only part of the reason why.

She was a striking woman who carried herself well. Lush curves, a lively, intelligent face, intricately braided hair the color of warm honey, a gracefully curved neck that almost begged a man to nuzzle just there. And her lips. Her lips looked like they would be soft as rose petals. He didn't know how long he'd been staring at her but when he finally pulled himself back out of his reverie, there was an amused, knowing look on her face that told him she knew exactly what he'd been thinking. Too bad he couldn't risk Sam getting too attached.

It was more honesty than he could afford to admit it was himself he was protecting.

Finn took the heavy cooler from her and motioned his head for Gustavia to lead the way. This time she gave in gracefully, letting him do the heavy lifting while she turned her attention to Sam.

Answering a new spate of rapid fire questions, she couldn't help thinking there was nothing to be seen of the shy girl from a year ago, Gustavia glanced back and caught Finn's eye with a twinkle in her own as she walked through the house and toward the patio.

Finn could only grin and shrug. It was going to be

hard work keeping her at arm's length, but today, he knew he was auditioning for a job and needed to be on his best behavior. Once in the backyard, he set the cooler down, greeted Julie and introduced his daughter.

"Everyone else will be along soon, Tyler needed to drop by and check on his grandfather and Amethyst stopped to pick up Kat," Julie informed Gustavia.

"Daddy, look at the gazebo, is it okay if I go sit in it?" She shifted from one foot to the other, eager to explore.

"Sure, Lola's down there now, let me call her and she can go with you, it's one of her favorite places and I know she's going to love meeting you."

Julie called out and within seconds, Lola came galumphing across the lawn. Finn couldn't help but chuckle, Lola running was a rare sight. She was not the most graceful of dogs but she was enthusiastic as head lowered and legs slightly akimbo, she ran full out, her back end trying to outrun her front.

Once she laid eyes on Sam, Lola altered course slightly and for a moment, it looked like she might run right over the girl, but she slid to a stop then looked up at Sam with brown eyes just begging for attention. Dropping to her knees, Sam drew the dog in for a hug and was rewarded with a gentle but sloppy kiss. Instant rapport.

"C'mon Lola, let's go for a walk," she called back to her father, "I'll be back."

Julie mistook the surprised look on his face for concern. "She'll be fine with Lola, I promise."

"No, it's not that. It's just—she doesn't usually get so comfortable so quickly when we go someplace new."

Gustavia exchanged a secretive smile with Julie,

"This place is special."

He let that pass.

"How do you think he's going to handle meeting Kat and Ammie?"

"I guess we will have to see. He laughed at my car, so maybe his mind isn't quite open enough. Oh, he tried to cover it up; he's a gentleman and all."

"Standing right here. Y'all treat everyone this way?" A little bit of Texas crept into his speech though he'd long since lost most of his drawl.

He faced two unrepentant grins. "Sometimes, it depends on the person and whether we think they have potential. Do you?"

"Have potential? Potential for what? I'm not exactly sure what's going on here." He felt out of his depth dealing with the banter. A non-existent social life meant it had been awhile since the last time he was lighthearted enough to participate in verbal gymnastics.

Until this very moment, he didn't realize how much he had missed it; missed feeling like the bottom wouldn't drop out from under him again if he so much as relaxed his guard for a minute. Holding himself back was frustrating, especially since he knew that these people could become friends if he could just let go of the fear produced by sudden loss.

A fear so powerful it dropped a shutter over him every time he felt the least urge to open up, let someone in besides Sam. That turned him short-tempered and rude.

Close the door on that, he thought.

He pulled his attention back to the present just in time to see Gustavia gesturing toward the house where her friend Amethyst, arm companionably draped over

Kat's shoulders, led the blind psychic onto the patio. Finn's eyes widened, then he let loose a low whistle.

Amethyst had that effect on people. Dressed in purple from head to toe; her hair and eyebrows were dyed a delicate shade of lavender giving her an ethereal, fairy-like appearance that was only enhanced by her diminutive height. With a grin, Gustavia said, "and you thought I dressed funny."

He tried to backtrack and say that he'd thought no such thing but she wasn't having any of it. "Oh, yes you do, but it's okay, I'll forgive you. Once." If that's what she thought, maybe it would be better to let her believe it. Telling her his bad behavior was brought on by panic because he was attracted to her and so was his daughter—well, better to let that slide by.

She could tell that he was trying to adjust and struggling with it a bit. He would either sink or swim and if he couldn't hang with the group, he couldn't hang with her. Just the way it was.

When Gustavia introduced him to the new arrivals and then to Tyler who'd been right behind them, he got another surprise. She might look like a tiny fairy but Amethyst's speaking voice, a deep, throaty purr, was anything but wraith-like.

Finn was glad to see another man and while Tyler manned the grill, the two of them made guy talk and watched the women.

"They do dazzle the eye, don't they?" Tyler chuckled at Finn's expression each time a burst of feminine laughter was heard. The man was obviously unused to being surrounded by a group of women with strong personalities.

"Bit much to take, seeing them all together like that,"

Finn commented with a shake of his head.

"Assume you mean that in a good way?" Tyler's mild mannered exterior housed a warrior soul. Derogatory comments would not be tolerated.

"Hmm? Oh, yes, absolutely." Tyler noted Finn's gaze might wander to the other three, but it was Gustavia who had him riveted. He kept the grin off his face but just barely. The signs were there, the guy was well on his way to being hooked.

"I got off on the wrong foot with her." Finn gestured toward Gustavia. "Now she thinks I'm a jerk."

"She's a free spirit, it puts some people off. But, under it all—the crazy clothes, the hair—there's solid. I won't tell you her story because it's not my place, but there is one and even with the solid, she has some fragile places."

It was a warning, gentle but clear and simple. To make his point, Tyler steeled his gaze. "She's Julie's and that makes her mine. Makes all of them mine, come to that."

Finn held up both hands. "I hear you. You protect what's yours. I admire that. It's not my intention to hurt her."

A former journalist, Tyler's people reading skills were tightly honed. Looking at Finn, he saw the misery, the fear and the wall the other man was trying to maintain. What he didn't see was any malice. He nodded and that was the end of it. They were square on the subject. For now.

Nodding his head toward the women, Finn ventured to ask, "Without telling me her story, what can you tell me about them? They seem tight."

"They are, and Gustavia's the glue. Kat's blind, you

could probably tell. She's a psychic and I know what you're going to say but I'll ask you to reserve judgment. She's the real thing. Trust me. Amethyst is an aura reader."

When Finn went bug-eyed, Tyler laughed. "Better you get that out of your system now, they won't appreciate disbelief if they see it on you. The auras are real, too, by the way. She's taught me to see them a little."

Another goggle-eyed look and Tyler shrugged. "Believe me or not, your choice. I only know what I've seen." The matter-of-fact statement left no room for debate.

"Gustavia writes, as you already know. And, she paints. She's a shrewd judge of character, generous to a fault and inventive. You should also be aware that she knows Krav Maga and while I have yet to see her bust out on anyone, Julie says she's good.

Now that the lines between them were drawn and understood, the two men moved to a lighter topic. Sports.

One ear on the conversation, Finn watched Sam in the gazebo as she played with Lola. He could see her talking to the dog and pretending to be a princess. She was an imaginative girl who enjoyed making up detailed stories and acting them out either alone or with her friends. He didn't see the spark of light hovering above the bench that lined the perimeter of the gazebo.

"MY LAST contractor didn't look like that," Amethyst whispered loudly. "He had a beer gut, a plumber's crack and wore suspenders attached to both his pants and his underwear. I guess I missed out."

"Shhh. He'll hear you, the male ego is a delicate creature, easily damaged, but feed it too much and you create a monster." Julie nearly snorted out her drink at Gustavia's dry comment.

"Tell us how you really feel," Kat teased.

"Are you going to hire him?" Gustavia turned to Julie.

"I'm leaning toward it if that's not a problem for you. He seems passionate about working on the house and it's not every day I run into someone who visited the museum."

Gustavia shrugged. "It's fine with me, do what you want. He's nice enough when he wants to be." Just not always to me.

SAMANTHA AND Lola rejoined the group and if his daughter was a little quieter than she'd been earlier, Finn put it down to her remembering she promised not to ask so many questions. She sat near Gustavia who treated her warmly, making sure she felt included and thought about what she'd seen in the gazebo.

At first, she had noticed Lola was acting funny, turning her head sideways as though she could hear something Sam couldn't. Sam knew dogs could hear better than humans, but this seemed different because she was also wagging her little stump of a tail so hard her entire body was shaking—but no one was there. Then, without warning, an older woman appeared right next to the happy dog.

Sam wasn't sure what to do next but she knew exactly what that prickling feeling was at the back of her neck. People didn't just pop up like that, she was seeing a spirit, a ghost. Creepy but still, the coolest thing ever.

Estelle hadn't been a resident of the hereafter for very long, so sometimes she unintentionally appeared in front of people. Usually, they couldn't see her anyway so it was no big deal, but when she'd heard the bell like sound of a young girl's voice in the gazebo, she'd become curious and the next thing she knew, she was facing Sam's wide-eyed gaze of astonishment. She should have remembered children were more sensitive.

"Who are you?" To her credit, Sam remained calm. A million questions flew into her head but, for once, she only asked the most important one.

"I'm Estelle, Julie is my granddaughter and this used to be my house. Don't be frightened, I mean you no harm."

"Oh, I'm not scared, not really. You look like a nice ghost. I just wasn't expecting you to pop up like that, it only freaked me out for a second, I'm not some kind of wimp. My name's Samantha but everyone calls me Sam, my dad's here to see about fixing the roof on your old house and I think he has a crush on Miss Gustavia."

Estelle smiled at the information dump. "Well, that's very nice and what do you think of Miss Gustavia?"

"She's the best. I love her books and the last one— my idea—well, sort of my idea. She dresses kind of funny sometimes, but I think she looks like a princess. Princess Gustavia. Did you know her when you lived here? Does she know you are still here? Can she see you?" No longer startled, Sam's usual spate of questions began to flow again.

"Indeed, I did. She was Julie's roommate in college

and then became part of our family. She is a very special person."

"I think so, too. Can I ask you something?" Sam's face took on a serious expression, eyes reflecting the troubled sadness that she always carried with her since the loss of her mother.

"You can ask me anything but there are some questions I am not allowed to answer." Sam nodded her head as though this made perfect sense.

"Does everyone who dies become a ghost? My mom died and if she is a ghost like you, why hasn't she come to see me?"

Estelle desperately wanted to say the right thing so she chose her words carefully. "I stayed here in order to help Julie with a task that she needed to complete, but soon, I will move on. Go into the light."

"Most people go there right away and I bet your mommy did, too."

Sam said nothing but her crestfallen look spoke volumes.

"I know you wish she could have stayed, even in spirit form, to watch you grow up and help you as much as she could, but I think you know that would have been the wrong thing to do. How sad would it be for her to see you but not be able to hug you when you need comfort or to kiss your cheeks? By moving on, she made space in your life for someone else to do those things, for someone else to love you. Not to take her place but just to add more to your life. She must have known that if she had stayed, you might not be as open to that and I can tell that you had a very wise and loving mommy."

"I don't want to forget her." Sam's tone echoed

misery and loss.

"No, of course you don't and you shouldn't. But, the best way you can remember her is by having a happy and loving life that becomes a tribute. Do you know what a tribute is?"

"I think I understand. It's like when Ember honored his mother in the story. Okay, but when you go to the light, if you see her, can you tell her I miss her?"

Estelle, overcome by emotion could only nod as she faded out of sight. Samantha sat quietly, petting Lola and pondering. Julie's grandmother was a nice ghost and her words had been comforting. If it was really okay to find another mommy, then Sam knew just the person for the job. Miss Gustavia.

Chapter Eight

Slathering his secret homemade barbecue sauce on several racks of ribs, Tyler hovered over the grill like a mother tending her baby while the girls put the rest of the meal together. Finn could see that this was not the first cookout the group had enjoyed; they were a well-oiled team who laughed and teased their way through each task. It was obvious that they were as close knit as most families yet he also felt the group's willingness to include him, the welcome that they extended to his daughter.

Lila had always been the social one, most of their friends started out as her friends first. Losing her had created enough of a disconnect for them to just naturally drift away leaving him isolated.

Gustavia set a platter piled high with corn in front of Kat who was sitting at the end of the table, then leaned down to quietly say, "There's a dozen ears, trash can's on your left, everything else is on your right." Kat smiled as she grabbed the first ear then turned toward Finn to explain, "They always stick me with the corn because I'm the only one who will pull off all the silk," before pulling back the husks to remove the offending strands.

When each ear was picked clean, she slathered it with softened butter then rolled it in a blend of spices before pulling the husks back into place and securing each one with a length of wet cooking twine. These were the next thing to hit the grill and now that everything else was almost ready, Tyler dropped a few slices of tofu beside the ribs and sauced them liberally as well.

Before he could stop her, Sam spoke up, "Is it because all of your other senses got stronger? We read about that in school."

"Sam, it's not appropriate to ask such personal questions. I'm sorry, she often speaks without thinking."

"It's fine." Kat turned in his direction. "Really, it is. Most of the time, people ignore my blindness because they're scared to ask questions, they think it will make me uncomfortable but those unasked questions eventually become a wall. One that makes it easier for people to start seeing me as *less than* instead of just different from them."

She turned back to the girl. "No, Samantha, my other senses are the same as before, but I do rely on them more since I lost my vision and most of the time that's a good thing." She smiled. "Like right now, I can tell you Amethyst made the potato salad because she uses just a pinch of celery salt in hers and I can smell it." She raised her voice, "And Tyler, the tofu is starting to scorch."

"That's so cool, it's like you have a super power." Just like that, she had put Sam at ease.

Finn frowned when Gustavia stifled a snort at Sam's comment. There was something going on here.

Something they were keeping from him. Nothing malicious, he just found it annoying to not be included.

He grabbed a soft drink from the cooler and poured Sam a cup of lemonade from the pitcher on the picnic table then, settling back into a deck chair, leveled a look at Gustavia.

"Spill it." He said pulling some folded papers from his shirt pocket and passing them to Julie. "This is my estimate. Just so you know, it's going to be lower than any you'll get because I want to work on your house and if it isn't, I'll go lower until you give me the job. I figure since that's the case and y'all seem so close, we're probably going to be spending some time together. So, you might as well tell me the story."

"What story?" Gustavia asked innocently.

"Whatever story you've been hinting at this whole time." He sat back waiting.

His pronouncement was greeted with a moment of silence before Amethyst said, "Every freaking time," and pulled a ten dollar bill from her pocket, handing it over to Kat. "You'd think I'd learn but I'm such a sucker."

Screams of laughter erupted around the table as Tyler also pulled out a ten and handed it to Julie. It was a long standing tradition that Ammie couldn't resist making them, but never won a bet with Kat and, as a lark, Julie had bet Tyler that money would change hands before the end of the day.

"What was it this time?"

"Five on whether Finn would get the job and the other five on whether we'd be telling him the story today." Amethyst mumbled.

Julie passed out plates with a pretty pattern of spring

flowers while the others began piling the rest of the food on platters. In a few short minutes, everyone was seated at the picnic table ready to eat.

Gesturing with his fork, Finn said, "Well, get on with it. What's going on? What's the big secret?"

"You ever see something that defies explanation?" Gustavia really wasn't expecting much.

"That's a pretty broad question. I've seen the sun set over the Grand Canyon, I watched Sam come into this world but I'm pretty sure that's not what you're asking. Be easier if you just say it right out. Speak plain."

Amethyst pushed a lock of lavender hair behind her ear, took a deep breath and jumped into the conversation. "I'm an aura reader, Kat's a psychic, Julie's been visited by the spirits of her grandmother and great grandfather and a month ago, we used the clues they gave us to find a key that led to a panel in her library where some of her family fortune had been hidden for years. That's how she can afford to repair the roof you're going to be working on. Any questions?"

Her gaze never wavered from his and she laid it out for him, her deep smoky voice taking on a bored tone. "No? There's more. Julie's ex, Logan, is a psychopathic con man with a deep hatred for both her and Gustavia. There are three more keys to find that we assume will lead to three more treasures and we never know when Logan will show up again." Still she maintained eye contact, "That plain enough?" There was no rancor in her tone, but she was curious to see what his reaction would be. He'd asked for plain speaking and that's exactly what she'd given him.

At first Gustavia thought he'd been rendered speechless by the revelation and she fully expected him to take back his estimate and leave. She was doomed to disappointment.

For several moments, the only noises to be heard were the sweet and persistent singing of the birds, the buzz and chirp of insects, while the entire table waited for him to speak.

Finn blinked several times, cleared his throat and said, "Treasure hunt? You had an actual treasure hunt?"

"Leave it to a guy to pick up on that part of it." Julie's dry tone was accompanied by a knowing smile. "And the rest of the story? Your thoughts?"

He wasn't about to tell them his thoughts since he was pretty sure saying it was a cockamamie story probably wouldn't land him the job and ghosts or no, he still wanted to be the one to bring this place back to glory. The roof was only the beginning. "Is it okay if I reserve judgment on that?"

Shrugs and grins were the only response he was going to get. If Gustavia chose not to act on her attraction, he'd probably finish the roof and stay uninvolved with the rest. Otherwise, he'd meet the ghosts eventually and see for himself. It was bound to happen since they tended to pop in without thinking. Unless he was one of those closed off people who could never see them. That would be the test.

"Now, tell me more about the hidden panel in the library. You have to show it to me. How does it work?"

Sitting quietly for once, Samantha struggled with whether or not she should mention meeting Estelle in the gazebo. It probably wasn't the best time to bring it up because she wasn't sure how her dad would take the news. But, she knew the others were telling the truth.

"HE'S NOT sure what to believe but I think he'll do. He's got potential." They all turned to see Estelle standing behind them as they watched Finn pull away down the drive.

"Potential for what?" Gustavia may have decided to give him the benefit of the doubt but she was still a bit annoyed with the man. He was inconsistent. Infuriating.

Estelle tilted her head and pinned the younger woman with a look. "This isn't the time to play coy. You know what I mean. There's a spark between you, you felt it and so did he."

"Maybe. But what if I want to throw water on the spark? Put it out before it starts a fire and burns down the town. Ever think of that?" It wasn't like Gustavia to sass Grams but her thoughts toward Finn were conflicted.

He was attractive, no doubt about that. He was gentle and loving with his daughter, she couldn't fault him there. But, then there was that side of him that just made her want to chew nails. The one she thought couldn't or wouldn't see past her exterior to the woman inside.

Wisely Estelle continued on, "The girl, she's very sweet and I should probably tell you that she can see me. It took me by surprise, too. We had a conversation in the gazebo."

"He'll probably blame that on me, too." Gustavia grumbled under her breath.

Estelle shot her another look. One that had Gustavia ducking her head and shuffling her feet.

Amethyst nudged Kat and whispered, "Ten?"

"Deal."

"Enough with this for now but be sure we will revisit the topic." Rarely had Estelle needed to resort to sternness, she'd raised Julie with much love and affection, but when the occasion demanded, she could be formidable.

"Now, update me. Any contact from Logan?"

"It's been a month; I bet he's halfway across the country and over it by now. Probably decided to cut his losses and move on. Forget all about us." Tyler said. "Can't Julius sense him anymore?"

Julius, just now appearing, answered the question with a troubled look on his face. "There's some kind of block or shield. I've been trying to find him but it's like he's become a black space."

Gustavia was thankful for the change of subject. She hated being on the receiving end of Estelle's displeasure but Finn came off as more than a little moody and she wasn't quite ready to trust him yet. He wasn't spiking her jerk meter the way Logan Ellis, had done, but he was messing with her senses. Until she had him pegged, she was keeping a bit of distance. Shame really, since he did have his moments and he came with a ready-made family. Something she longed to have for herself.

Hearing the mention of her brother's name pulled her focus back to the conversation.

"Zack keeps us informed but there have been no reported sightings for the past couple weeks. Zack figures he's gone to ground somewhere. Changed his name, probably his appearance, too. Current theory is that he will probably resurface at some point. Somewhere far away from here, though"

"The man is well on his way to being insane, I'm worried about you. Promise me you will all be vigilant,

I still have a bad feeling about him."

A scowling Julius intoned, "Best thing all around is to continue on to the next step. I have a theory it's all tied together, your hunt and that young man's sanity."

"Are you allowed to tell us anything helpful this time?" Tyler asked.

He thought for a minute then his scowl deepened.

"You already have the key but I can't tell you what it is."

"Cryptic as always."

CHAPTER NINE

Tyler was only partly right, Logan was halfway across the country but he hadn't forgotten the humiliation handed to him when Gustavia nearly caught him in her little booby trap. A month later and he was still seething. He'd managed to pull himself enough to move on to the next con but this one wasn't going well, either. Defeat had robbed him of his edge, his ability to blend into the corporate crowd. It had left a visible stain on him, he was tainted with it and he blamed Gustavia. She was the one. She had poisoned Julie against him and then, even worse, set her cop brother on his tail.

Now he couldn't seem to fit back into his old life, the one where he'd been suave enough, believable enough, to sell anything to anyone.

When he looked in the mirror, he still saw that man, the ultimate actor, the con artist. He didn't see the dangerous light in his own eyes, the barely restrained fury or the condescending attitude that visibly labeled everyone around him a mark.

Caught in the web of self-denial, he didn't understand that his arrogance and disdain was written all over him. It was there in the way he carried himself, in the way he spoke. There was nothing left in him of the patience required for running another long con, he'd give himself another week to make some headway and unless he saw some progress, he'd be forced to turn his attention toward revenge. They would pay, every one of them and Gustavia most of all.

Satisfied his decision was the best one, Logan finished shaving, got dressed and left the hotel. He hadn't seen any reason to rent a condo this time, he was only planning to be in town for a week or so before the next stage of the plan either saw him relocating entirely or returning to Oakville.

The sun shone from an impossibly blue sky, throwing heat shimmers off the roof as bare-chested men with bunching muscles hammered new sheathing in place. Gustavia, Julie and Amethyst watched with growing appreciation as heat-teased sweat made masculine bodies glimmer and shine.

"It's nice here in the gazebo." Gustavia fanned herself lazily, lips quirked in appreciation at the view.

"Think we're participating in some sort of reverse objectification ritual? Like when construction workers yell sexual slurs at passing women?" Amethyst idly wondered aloud.

"We haven't yelled any sexual slurs...yet." Julie waggled her eyebrows.

"Oh look, that one dropped his hammer—that's right, bend over, pick it up—and there it is."

"Hey, we were just congratulating ourselves for not stooping."

"Well, I didn't yell it did I? Don't I get a little credit

for a sotto voce violation of the sexual objectification code?" Gustavia grinned then repeated. "It's nice here in the gazebo."

"I believe this moment needs immortalizing." Julie levered out of her chair and sauntered back toward the house returning minutes later with her camera. She fitted it with a nice long lens and sat back, aiming and snapping away.

Kat seriously considered calling on Estelle to provide her with a set of eyes.

Resigned to a life of darkness until she channeled Julie's grandmother, it had come as a great shock when her sight returned while Estelle had come through. Not a fluke, it had happened every time and it was tempting to overuse the privilege but, while ogling hot construction workers would be nice, she didn't feel it was important enough a reason to ask for that kind of help. Still, she knew she was missing out

Up on the roof, Finn's eyes behind a pair of tinted safety glasses kept straying to the group of girls lounging in the gazebo. They made a sight, the four of them stretched out on lawn chairs, chatting and drinking lemonade but every time he glanced over, it was Gustavia who pulled his focus. Whatever she'd braided into her hair today glittered in the sun like the halo of an angel. Come to think of it, considering what she'd done for his daughter, she probably deserved the description.

Still, looking at the long, lightly tanned legs she was showing off today, his thoughts were leaning toward more devilish pursuits. He wanted her. Plain and simple. And that wanting scared him to death so he was determined to get over it. Avoiding her would be the best way to handle his attraction. In time, he would forget her. That was the plan. Best to stick to the plan.

Yet, not even half an hour later, he strolled toward the gazebo and invited her to come up and take a look at his crew's progress.

"Funny, that," Amethyst commented to Julie as the pair of them walked away. "It's your house but she's the one checking over the work." She sat up, watching, trying to judge by their body language whether things were heating up or cooling down. Julie grinned.

Kat said soberly, "I think he might be the one from her reading, the one with all the baggage. Her soul mate. Did she tell you she has one?"

Amethyst mused, "Her aura is off color. His, too. I'm thinking they might be in for a bit of a rough start to their relationship."

"Her cards show a rocky path leading to a crossroads; one path leads to true love, the other to a lifetime alone. It's major."

"Can we do anything? Without making it worse." Julie asked.

"Not sure yet. For now, we wait and watch. That goes for you too, Estelle." Kat sensed the spirit's presence just before she became visible.

"I wasn't planning to meddle, young lady." Estelle said with a smile in her voice. "I'll leave that up to the living." She mused, "They remind me of magnets turned pole to pole. What should attract just repels, but flip one of them and it's hard to pull them apart." Then, she glanced at Ammie and asked, "Got any bets running on which one will flip?" All she got for an answer was a faked expression of innocence, one that raised a smile before she faded softly away again.

"I'd think about getting in on that action but it's too

close to call." Julie raised her camera, focused in on Gustavia and Finn's heads bent toward each other as they earnestly discussed some aspect of roofing and snapped several shots.

CHAPTER TEN

When Gustavia's phone rang later that evening, she was shocked to see Finn's name on the screen. After a moment's hesitation, she decided to see what he wanted.

"It's Finn," he said when she'd answered. Then silence stretched out for a moment.

"Is everything okay?" What did he want? "Is it Sam?"

"No, she's fine. I just wanted to talk to you and now that I've called, I don't know what to say. Can we just chat for a few minutes?"

Over the phone, his softly pitched voice sounded comforting, like home. The gentle hint of a drawl soothed and excited at the same time.

"Okay, sure. Tell me how you got into restoration work." It seemed like a safe enough subject.

"It was my mother, believe it or not. When I was a kid, we went to Newport, Rhode Island on vacation and she dragged us through the mansion tours. She was so excited. The architecture, the bones of the structures—amazing, then they gilded the lily with the most intricate trim work. The moldings were like a giant puzzle and I could see how it all fit together, one piece stacked on another. Something just clicked and that was it for me."

"Sounds nice."

"What about you? Why children's books?"

She thought for a minute and instead of the pat answer she normally gave to interviewers, she told him the naked truth.

"Escape. It was something I needed when I was a child and I found it in books. Edward Eager, E. Nesbitt, Madeleine L'Engle, Oz, Alice in Wonderland, Narnia. Those authors, worlds and characters were my refuge, my family. Eventually, I progressed to creating my own worlds, ones where I had all the power. Writing those books set me free."

It was more honesty than she normally offered. "Your mother sounds like a gem." There was the merest whisper of envy in her voice.

"She is."

Another silence and this time Gustavia let it spin out. He was the one who called her; let him come up with something to talk about.

"Tell me something true, something about you."

She thought for a moment. "I'm addicted to Pixie Stix."

He laughed. "That candy stuff in a straw? That's pretty much pure sugar."

"I know. It's like crack. I crave them. Your turn."

"I still like to stomp mud puddles. I pretend I'm doing it with Sam, but I'd still do it if she wasn't around and I knew no one was looking."

"I have a huge Lego collection."

"Me, too. They're in Sam's room but I play with them whenever I can."

"Couple of true grown-ups."

"My mother always said that childish and childlike were two entirely different concepts."

"Words to live by."

Silence, this time comfortable, peaceful.

"Goodnight Gustavia."

"Hmm. 'Night Finn."

Shaking her head, she clicked to end the call. Well, that was interesting, she thought, and totally unexpected. The superman reference might not have been so far off, by night he was mild mannered Finn Kent who occasionally, by day, turned into Loserman.

With a smile on her face and that thought in her head, Gustavia got ready for bed.

Kat felt a bit out of place at a photo shoot, even when it was being held at a friend's house. She couldn't see the models, couldn't help with the setups like Amethyst and Gustavia but she appreciated being included. Today's designer was an up and comer whose clothes were exquisitely eclectic, so she was told.

Amethyst lived in a charming underground home behind a spectacularly carved doorway set into a hill above the lake. It was the perfect setting for the shoot and Julie had practically begged to have it there, sweetening the deal by inviting her friends to watch and help with the process.

Of course, the location fee that more than covered a regular day's worth of clients hadn't hurt either.

At the outset, Kat tried to decline since it was a visual experience and she didn't want to be in the way. Or to inspire pity. Her friends were having none of it.

Though they didn't share it with her, the other three had a theory that exposing her to these types of outings might provide some added incentive to either lose or let go of the fear causing her blindness. Plus, everything was more fun when they were all together.

It was an early shoot, really early. Since Amethyst's front door faced east and was near enough the lake for frequent morning mists, Julie had dragged them all there at what Gustavia called "the plumber's crack of dawn".

Now, five hours later, the models and stylists were just leaving.

"That went really well, I think. And I loved the clothes." Gustavia helped Julie pack up her equipment. She was an old hand at the process, having assisted Julie on plenty of shoots. Now, with Julie branching out from art photography to fashion, she enjoyed seeing the difference in the two processes.

Once everything was packed and stowed in Julie's car, the four friends sat around the table sipping cups of tea.

After they had exhausted all fashion related topics, and with a wicked twinkle in her eye, Amethyst skewered Gustavia with a question. "So, what's the deal with you and the mighty Finn?"

Gustavia only snorted. "No clue. Too bad, though. He'd probably be tasty if he wasn't so testy."

"Har har. That's funny."

Shrugging her shoulders, Gustavia smirked. "One minute he's charming, the next he's snarky, then he acts like nothing happened. Next thing I know, he calls me and we talk for half an hour exchanging true stories. I'm not exactly sure what to expect next, but since he sometimes gives off an unstable vibe, I'll pass."

"Maybe the snark wasn't personal, maybe he was just having an off day that first time," was Kat's opinion. "You can be intimidating at times."

"So how am I supposed to know? It sure felt personal to me."

"Just ask him." It was a chorus of all three voices.

"Just ask him? That's all you've got? A psychic, an aura reader and a newly engaged woman and this is the best advice you have for me? Just ask him. Truly impressive."

"No one said you had to listen, but you did ask." Julie had only ever seen Gustavia flash into this contrary a mood when dealing with her family or with Logan.

"You're usually more open than this, what's different with Finn? That's the big question, here." Kat mused. "Why does his opinion matter so much?"

"It doesn't matter. I just hate it when people jump to conclusions about me like that. Plus, he used the word flounce, incorrectly I might add since it means to basically storm off in a huff. I think he meant to say prance. Not that prancing is any better."

Amethyst raised an eyebrow at that. "You've had a little exercise in the jumping to conclusions area lately. Hence the advice to ask him point blank what he thinks. Get it out in the open."

"Yeah, hence."

Gustavia wrinkled her nose. "So I ask him and he says he thinks I am a new age wing nut with bad dress sense. Then what? I buy new clothes? Or worse, I don't buy anything new—ever—just to make a point. See my dilemma?"

"It's a question. There's give and take in every relationship but I'm not so sure that's what this is all about. I've known you a long time, longer than anyone else in the room, and I've seen you use your clothes as a sort of armor against your family's rejection."

Gustavia opened her mouth to protest but Amethyst held up a hand, shaking her head, "No, let me finish, this is important. You needed a visual reminder to show them you're not like them and never will be. But, sometimes you use it as an excuse not to get close to people. If they don't accept you based on a first impression, you decide they aren't worth the time. I'm not sure that's entirely fair."

"Ammie, have you looked in a mirror recently? Coming from you, that statement seems just ludicrous."

Kat and Julie stayed silent. Neutral. Safer that way.

"Well, I'm not the one getting all kerfluffled about some guy, and I'll be the first to admit that I can recognize it in you because I see that same tendency in myself. But, I know we aren't coming from the same pain. I can't pretend to understand what being rejected by family might feel like, mine loves me no matter what and it hurts me to know that yours doesn't."

She felt such a welling of sympathy for Gustavia who had been carrying this pain with her for so long.

Kat broke her silence to say, "Frankly, I don't much care whether he has an opinion on your personal style and I don't think you do either. I do think you care very much what he thinks of you, the person under the clothes. If he is the catalyst that helps you deal with your past, your family, it's another factor."

She continued thoughtfully, "I'd even be willing to bet he is using the idea of protecting Sam as his own brand of armor."

For once, Amethyst declined to put her money on the line.

"How much does Samantha figure into this?" Julie knew there'd been an instant connection with the girl; it had been easy for Gustavia to relate to someone who had lost a parent when she felt she'd lost both of her own.

"I fell in love with her from day one. She's such a bright spirit but underneath, there's this immense loss she's struggled so hard to handle. Courage. She has it in spades. But, if it's going to keep throwing me off balance. I'm thinking that it would be better to just stay away from both of them."

That pronouncement was met with three identical looks of skepticism that Gustavia then returned with narrowed eyes.

"Romance is supposed to throw you off balance," Amethyst pronounced.

In theory, Gustavia agreed but she thought romance was supposed to feel good, not dredge up every bit of pain from the past.

Trying to lighten the mood, Julie changed the subject.

"It's still early. Are your schedules free for the rest of the day? What do you say we all go back to my place and ogle the construction guys some more? Well, maybe not you, Gustavia, since you want to stay away from Finn." It was a challenge, plain and simple.

"Oh, I'm in. There will be no ogling without me."

CHAPTER ELEVEN

Living in a smaller town had its advantages. Logan Ellis, with his arrogant manner, hadn't made any friends in Oakville, so when word got around that he was on the wanted list, people paid attention even when they went into the nearby city. Pete, the owner of the grocery store, was in the warehouse district for an appointment with one of his suppliers when he saw Logan walking into a public storage facility. He did the right thing.

He called Zack who did some digging and found that a unit had been rented under the name Kyle Logan. Bingo. He sent the updated information through channels and requested increased police presence near the storage unit. With every cop in the city keeping an eye out, the chances of catching this scumbag increased dramatically.

Once things were set in motion, he dialed in Tyler's number.

"Ty, it's Zack Roman. I wanted to give you a head's up, Ellis was spotted in the city this morning."

"Too much to hope that he'd left for good, I suppose. We'll keep an eye out on our end and we've all got you on speed dial. You going to tell your sister or do you want us to handle it?" He was aware of the tension between the siblings.

"I'll talk to her. It's been easier to do that lately."

"Good. She's quite something, our Gustavia. What's your gut telling you? Which one is he going to target, Julie or Gustavia?"

"It's fifty-fifty in my opinion. Maybe both if he can manage it. Way I see it, he won't go after Julie at the house. Not with Lola in residence and after his last experience. He'll think Gustavia's the more vulnerable of the two. Probably doesn't know she's got a state of the art alarm system," he speculated.

Tyler murmured his agreement.

"My biggest concern is that he might try to grab her, use her as leverage against Julie, then he'd have them both."

"Depends on his end game I guess."

Tyler pointed out, "That bit with Lola did the job when he tried to get in here before. Stroke of genius."

When Julie had refused to install an alarm system, Gustavia had rigged up a booby trap for Logan. One that had netted him a nasty bite from the normally friendly Lola. "The woman has a devious mind. Gotta admire her for it. We've got a line on a way to balance the scales. I'll let you know if it works out. Friend of a friend has a dog that needs a home."

"And Julie thought of Gustavia. Bit of female retaliation?"

Tyler chuckled. "Maybe a little. But it seems like a good idea to me, too. He's a smaller dog, a Jack Russell Terrier, but the owner says he is mighty despite his size and good company on top of it."

"I'll call her about Ellis and keep mum about the dog.

No sense in spoiling the surprise."

"Or getting moved back to the top of her list," Tyler teased, before they ended the call.

Still, despite the attempt to lighten the conversation, he dreaded telling Julie that Logan was in the area again. They'd all hoped the trouble with him was over, but clearly that wasn't the case. The man was determined to get revenge.

JULIE AND AMETHYST pulled out behind Gustavia and Kat in her Maverick and they began to drive down the hill. As they rounded the first curve, the Maverick seemed to pick up speed, pulling away. That's odd, Julie thought. Maybe Gustavia really was angry with us for offering advice.

That was not the problem. Something was wrong. Terribly wrong. When Gustavia punched the brakes going into the curve, they went to the floor with no resistance at all. She tried pumping them and still nothing.

The Maverick sped into the next curve as Gustavia fought the wheel. "Oh, Kat, we're in trouble," she yelled, "The brakes are gone."

It was a good thing she had taken a defensive driving course so she had at least a rudimentary idea of what to do. Dropping the shifter into low helped reduce the momentum slightly but given the steepness of the hill, she was still fighting to keep the car in the road. It took most of her concentration and the quick work of both hands on the wheel to maintain enough control to stop the car from pitching down over one of the steep drop offs.

A quick test of the parking brake told her it, too was disabled.

The road curved along the side of the hill above the lake for a half mile or so before sloping more sharply downward into a series of shorter, sharper, s-shaped curves. The car was still picking up speed as the road steepened for the last two curves.

Julius and Estelle, called by her fear, arrowed toward Gustavia and the Maverick. Combining their energy, the two spirits produced a barrier. It didn't slow the car by much but it was the best they could do and they hoped it was enough. The burst of energy depleted both their reserves leaving them powerless to do more than watch what happened next.

Dimly, Gustavia became aware of the shrieking from the tires as she rounded the next bend in the road and knew the worst was yet to come. There was one final curve coming up before the road straightened for the last long run into town. The slope leveled out into a long flat section of road where she would be able to slow down before she barreled through the village but first, she had to make that last curve.

Gaining momentum slightly, the Maverick held to the road around the tightest section of the curve but with a sinking feeling, Gustavia felt the tires break free as she hit a small patch of gravel just before she could straighten out. The car, thrown from the pavement, careened down the shallow embankment, fishtailing as she tried to steer through clumps of grass hoping to slow the car. Her plan worked well enough that when they passed through a shallow thicket of underbrush and bumped into a large pine tree, the car was already nearly stopped.

Neither woman spoke at first, then Gustavia reached over and grasped Kat's hand. "It's over, are you okay? Are you hurt?"

"I don't think so." She took a deep breath, then took stock. "I think I'm going to have a couple of bruises."

Gustavia unfastened her seat belt and wrenched the door open, her first thought was to help Kat, get to her side of the car and assess any injuries. She barely registered the mounting ache in her head where at some point that she didn't even remember, it had connected with the side window.

Kat's door was wedged against a small rock but that wasn't going to stop her. Using a dead branch, Gustavia levered the rock out of the way, all the time reassuring her friend, and yanked open the door. Dropping to her knees, she checked Kat for signs of trauma and finding none, helped her out of the car.

Sounds came slowly back as the adrenalin rush began to subside. With a moan of despair, she slumped down on a nearby fallen tree pulling Kat down to sit beside her, and began to cry.

"Gustavia, oh my God. Are you okay? Kat, say something." Julie and Amethyst came crashing through the brush with anxious faces.

"We're okay," Kat replied, her voice trembled then strengthened. "We're okay."

"You scared the life out of us. What happened."

"The brakes, it was the brakes. I saw Julius and Estelle, they did something to help slow the car then they were gone." Gustavia's hands shook as she reached up to gingerly probe the side of her head, the ache was getting worse.

"Let me look," Julie gently brushed the hair back to

see a sizable lump. "She's hurt." Julie said pulling her phone from her pocket to see if there was service. Full bars. She called the paramedics, then she called Gustavia's brother Zack.

"I'm fine, it's just a little bump. There's no need to call in the cavalry."

"You're shaking like a leaf, you're getting checked out by the paramedics and Zack is a cop. He's going to find out anyway, don't you think the news is better coming from me than over the police scanner. He cares about you no matter what you think."

"I know, I know. Spare me the lecture. I've got a headache already."

Amethyst contacted Kat's family to let them know what had happened and reassure them.

Finally, Julie called Tyler as she could already hear sirens in the distance.

Zack Roman was the first to arrive and Julie knew she'd been right to call him. For once, he was tender with his sister. Gesturing for Julie to move aside, he sat beside Gustavia, put his arm around her and held on. Her eyes went wide, surprised, when she realized he, too was trembling slightly. He cared. Deep inside, she'd always known he did, but it was nice to see it in his eyes.

He said nothing, but after a few moments, took a deep breath, gave her a squeeze and then went over to the car to take a look at it.

"The damage doesn't look too bad, sis. What happened?"

"The brakes failed." She shuddered as she relived the moment she'd felt the pedal slide to the floor with no resistance. "I could have been killed—we could have been killed. Oh, Kat. I'm so sorry. I just had the car in for its yearly check, and the mechanic said she was in fine shape. I had no idea. You must have been so scared."

"It all happened so fast, I didn't have enough time to be scared until it was pretty much all over but I knew we were going to be fine. Spirit told me to stay calm."

Zack's eyes narrowed as suspicion entered his mind. He knelt on the ground to check under the car. In its present position, he couldn't tell if the brakes had been tampered with but he followed his instincts, called in a favor and had a trusted mechanic pick up the car and instructed him to give it the once over then call him with the results.

When the paramedics arrived, they confirmed that other than a few bumps and bruises, Kat was fine but Gustavia probably had a minor concussion so she got to ride with them to the ER.

Julie and the other women, followed by Zack in his cruiser, made the trip behind the ambulance while Tyler stayed behind, under Zack's orders, to supervise the tow truck. He would meet the others once the car was hauled away.

Gustavia was treated and released, the knot on her head requiring ice and painkillers, was not a concussion. She had been very lucky.

Arriving back at Julie's house, they found Finn waiting for them. After his crew called it a day, he hadn't wanted to leave the house unsecured so he stayed. At least that's what he told himself. It had nothing to do with Gustavia's being hurt and his intense need to see firsthand just how badly. To make sure she was alright.

Unable to just stand around and do nothing, he'd gone inside and, hoping Julie would forgive him for the intrusion, raided her pantry to put together a batch of cookies. His mother had passed along her habit of using baking as a method to relieve stress. There was something calming about measuring and mixing ingredients and the activity kept his mind from wandering. When Julie texted him that neither woman had been badly injured and that they expected to be back within the hour, Finn was finally able to relax a little and allow some of the tension to leave his body.

And, when he saw Gustavia walk through the door a little banged up but whole, he couldn't, wouldn't admit it, but he felt the urge to leap for joy.

Gratefully munching on a homemade cookie, Gustavia, leaving out the part about seeing Julius and Estelle, went over the story one more time. Though, by the end of her recitation she was looking a little pale.

Finn noticed her flagging energy and said, "Samantha's having her first sleepover birthday party. I'd just be going home to an empty house." He seemed slightly unnerved at the prospect. "Let me take you home, get you settled in and I'll even cook dinner."

Hadn't she said, just this morning, that she thought seeing him was a bad idea? Seeing him without the buffer of Samantha? Worse idea. Absolutely not. The answer was no—just no.

So, naturally, she said, "Yes."

DRIVING TOWARD Gustavia's home for the first time, Finn wondered what to expect. She was quiet. After the ordeal she'd been through, he wasn't surprised. He was impressed with the way she'd handled herself. Only her quick thinking kept the accident from turning deadly.

He'd keyed her address into his GPS and when he turned down her street, he knew without being told exactly which house was hers; the charming one constructed from what looked like a jumble of additions. Cedar shake siding weathered to a silvery gray below a modified, hipped roof whose corners had been rounded to provide the feel of a thatched cottage.

There was almost no lawn in front because the entire yard was an artfully designed garden. There were primrose-lined stone paths leading through plantings designed to attract butterflies. On the far side of the house was a gate leading to the back yard, over the gate arched a simple arbor. Beautiful purple Clematis climbed its trellised sides. It was lovely.

"Great house. It suits your personality."

Distracted with wondering what on earth had caused her to agree to this, Gustavia mumbled, "Mmhm."

"How's the head? Are you in pain?" She seemed very distant, not herself. Understandable but all the same, he was concerned.

She pulled her attention back with an effort. "No, the painkillers are working. Are you sure you want to stay? I feel fine. Really. "

Not really, he thought. Not fine at all. Worried and a little annoyed, maybe. But not fine. No way was he leaving her alone until she was more settled. Sam would kill him if anything happened to Miss Gustavia. Right now, it was his job to see that nothing did. "I'll stay. I want to." He insisted despite her skeptically arched eyebrow and sidelong glance.

She shrugged. Whatever. He'd better keep a lid on

the snark this time, she wasn't in the mood. It had been a long day already as she unlocked the door gesturing for him to step inside while she dealt with the security system. She hated the thing but after today, she might have to rethink that position.

Logan, if he was behind this, and she was pretty sure he was, had clearly been bold enough to cut the brake lines on her car in broad daylight. She had to face the truth, he'd tried to hurt her, maybe kill her. Without being told, she knew those were Zack's suspicions and she also knew his instincts were correct.

Tomorrow she'd call Zack and thank him for making her install the stupid alarm; it wouldn't kill her to be nice to him. Not after seeing how rattled he'd been at the scene today. That had been quite the surprise.

While her thoughts were otherwise occupied, she realized Finn had been speaking and she had no idea what he'd said. "Sorry, I'm a little distracted. It's been a long day."

That was obvious, he thought, considering the visible strain around her eyes. Her normally luminous skin was pale.

"Just point me toward the kitchen, you'll feel better once you've eaten something more substantial than a cookie. Not that my cookies are wimpy."

A hint of a twinkle finally reached her eyes, "Can you cook?"

"I am a man of many skills." he stated as he followed her into the kitchen and while she put on a pot of water for tea, rummaged through the fridge to see what was there to work with.

It was too late to avoid this situation so she might as well at least try to relax and enjoy it, take this opportunity to get him out of her system.

"So, what are we having tonight? The typical dude's go-to? An omelet?"

"You think so little of me? Please." Taking mock offense and pulling ingredients from the fridge he asked, "What kind of herbs are in your planting beds?"

"How do you know I grow herbs?"

Raising an eyebrow, he waved a hand to indicate it was a foolish question. She pointed to the sliding glass doors, "See for yourself, through the doors, down the path and to the left."

If her front yard was lovely, it paled in comparison to the back yard. He found a variety of herbs planted in well-mulched, tiered beds. Mature trees, bushes and shrubs provided shade for those plants that thrived in lower sun conditions, vegetable beds nestled next to complimentary plantings of flowers. It was meticulously planned to provide enough produce for the table as well as an oasis of peace. He snipped a bit of thyme, rosemary, some tarragon and a few sprigs of parsley, then, seeing she had already begun harvesting small potatoes from a contained bed, he pulled six or so of the small, red gems from the dirt.

Back in the kitchen, he scrubbed the potatoes, coated them with the fragrant extra-virgin olive oil she kept in a container beside the range, sprinkled them with parsley and tarragon and popped them in the oven. While they were roasting, he preheated the cook top grill, mixed together his favorite blend of seasonings then rubbed it into a couple chicken cutlets and set them to grilling. Next, he sliced two rashers of bacon into a sauté pan. After cooking it to tender crisp, he pulled out the bacon, added crushed garlic then tossed in a handful of green beans, some almonds he found in a jar in the cupboard and at the end, finished the dish with a splash of balsamic vinegar and added back in the bacon.

It wasn't an omelet. Gustavia was impressed and realized she actually was hungry.

"Okay, you're good," her appreciative tone only slightly tinged with surprise.

"It isn't polite to say *I told you so*, so I'll refrain. But it won't be easy. The temptation to rub it in is nearly overwhelming." His teasing smile made her heart skip a beat. Maybe his behavior the other day had been an aberration. She started to relax and enjoy the conversation.

He talked about how the roof was coming along, described how some of the transitions from one style of architecture to the other created challenges for his crew and how they solved them.

His voice, slightly husky and with that faint Texas flavor was soothing to her nerves and he seemed to understand that she was still a little frazzled.

There'd been precious little time for her to process the events of the day, the danger she'd faced and still might. As he continued to talk and she relaxed into the sound, her eyes filled with tears that finally spilled down her face as she started to shake.

Falling silent, he reached across the breakfast bar where they were seated and took her hand, absentmindedly brushing his fingers across her soft skin. The silent shaking turned to sobs as emotions overwhelmed her.

"I could've killed her," she wailed. "Oh, my God, she could have died and it would have been all my fault."

Keeping hold of her hand, he rounded the end of the

bar and pulled her into his arms. "Shhh, honey," he whispered against her hair. "Kat's fine. You're fine. You were amazing, you handled it, the car, everything. You kept her safe. It's over now."

"It happened so fast, I didn't have time to think, but now I can't stop thinking about it. It keeps replaying in my mind; the scream of the tires, the guard rail flashing past, and that tree rushing at me."

He didn't know what else to do so he lowered his head and brushed her lips with his. Just the merest touch at first, then as though some invisible bond keeping them apart finally snapped, they dived into the kiss and it heated up to smoking hot in an instant. Her hands speared into his hair as he crushed her close, then closer still.

Her breath mingled with his as she sighed against his lips, returning kiss for kiss.

All he could think at first was how right this felt, how perfectly she fit against him. His body tensed into fight or flight mode, tightening his gut as he fought to tame both fear and elation. Just the merest whisper of a voice in his mind said, "Yes, please, go and be happy." The voice sounded like Lila.

No—he answered—not yet, I'm not ready.

Gustavia wasn't crying now. She wasn't even thinking. Lost in the sensation of his lips as the touch of them loosened everything inside of her, she gave herself without reservation until he slowly pulled back, resting his forehead against hers.

"I didn't want to do that." It was exactly the wrong thing to say.

"Then why did you?" Eyes firing, her spine stiffened and she flattened her palms against his chest pushing him forcefully away. A moment too late he remembered she could probably kick his butt. "You've been giving off mixed signals since just about day one. What is your deal? Is it me in particular or are you just one of those guys?" The scathing tone of her voice was sharp enough to cut glass.

Anger crowded out everything else, she could have spit nails.

"It's not personal." And it wasn't. Not really. He was only trying to protect his daughter. To keep her from getting too attached to a woman who might not stay part of her life.

Everything in him wanted to sweep Gustavia off her feet, to be her knight in shining armor, carry her off to his castle forever.

Okay, he didn't have a castle, he had a duplex next the Laundromat, but the intention was still the same. He just couldn't shake the dreaded feeling that he would have to watch his daughter sink into the dark place again if he brought another woman into her life. Look how close she had come today. A little less skill, a bit more loose gravel on the road, a car coming the other way and she would have been gone. Just like that. Just like Lila.

Sam was already too deeply involved. He had to put a stop to it. Now. It never occurred to him it was his own heart he was trying to protect.

Gustavia saw something flicker through his eyes, a memory, a ghost from the past. Okay, so he had his own demons. Everybody did. It didn't matter, though. He was rejecting her and using the old—it's not you, it's me—line to do it. Sure, it was personal, and she got it, his wife died in a car accident, she'd just had a car accident, it had to be bringing up those memories. Made perfect sense. A few kisses weren't enough to overcome his deep fear. She felt sorry for him, sorry for herself and sorry for Sam.

"Gustavia, I—I don't know what to say."

She said nothing, torn between one more rejection and her sense of empathy; she realized there was no middle ground, no place for them to meet.

Looking away, she waited for him to leave.

CHAPTER TWELVE

Zack's mechanic had already given him the good news/bad news situation.

The good news: the damage was repairable. Old cars with metal frames generally stood up to trees better than their newer counterparts.

The bad news: the brake lines had been cut, the parking brake tampered with. Someone had tried to hurt his sister.

No doubt in his mind, Logan Ellis was back. Julie's ex-fiancé blamed Gustavia when his scam on Julie fell through. Zack turned the car over to forensics hoping the jerk had left something, some shred of evidence he could use to nail him.

There was another good news/bad news moment to all this.

The good news: about two seconds after Julie broke the news he realized how much his sister meant to him.

The bad news: now he had to talk to her about the situation. Nothing to look forward to, but better to get it over with sooner rather than later.

Typically male, Zack preferred to avoid any situation where he had to admit he'd been wrong. Worse when he wasn't sure what kind of reception that admission might get.

It was time to eat crow.

He parked in front of her place and sat in his car for a moment trying to work through the words he knew he needed to say. He owed his sister an apology, had for years now.

Sitting in the car wouldn't get it done, so, much as he dreaded the next few minutes, he made his way toward the house. Zack lifted his hand to knock on the door just as it opened and a man he'd never met pulled it open and stalked out, nodding his head curtly and continuing down the walkway.

Out of curiosity, he turned and watched the man who made it to the sidewalk before he looked back and saw Zack watching him. He stopped and called back, "I'm Finn Kent."

"Zack Roman," was the response, "I'm her brother." That last was said pointedly as he wondered who Finn was to his sister and what his intentions were.

Finn walked back and extended his hand. "Look, man. She's some woman but you already know that." He started to walk away again. Then turned back. "God, she gets under my skin. She makes me crazy." Zack nodded solemnly while inside he was grinning from ear to ear.

If he wasn't mistaken, his sister was either in a relationship or soon would be. The signs were crystal clear; the guy was in over his head. Straightening his shoulders, Finn nodded then nodded again, turned and walked away. This time he kept going.

Allowing the grin to surface for a moment, then stifling it, Zack knocked on the door.

"You really need to leave, Finn," Gustavia called through the door.

"It's not Finn." Seconds passed before the door swung open.

Zack could see bruises blossoming on his sister's pale skin. At that moment, he was torn between an equally strong desire to reach out and hold her and another to track down the man who had put those marks on her and kill him. Not appropriate thinking for an officer of the law. He swallowed heavily. "Can I come in?"

"Sure, sorry. I was just surprised and it's been an incredibly long day. My head's a little fuddled." She stepped back giving him space to come through the door while thinking he looked upset.

"Who's the guy?"

"Finn? No one." He was someone, no mistake. But he let it go.

"Eloise." She just stared at him until he gave in. "Gustavia, then. We need to talk."

"Okay." What was coming? It sounded ominous.

He dropped his head in his hands. Now she was scared. "What is it? Is it mom or dad?"

"No, you fool. It's you. You scared me half to death. When Julie called, I thought I'd lost you. Puts everything in perspective, you know? There are things I've never said, things I need to say." He fell silent while he pulled his thoughts together. Gustavia merely waited. She was wary of what he might say and more than a little nervous.

Wishing she had a cup of tea to smooth out the anxiety, she let him begin.

"I'm sorry. I know it may be too little, too late but I

have to tell you. I let things happen because it was easier than standing up for myself—or for you. When they sent us away without warning, then took me back—well, I should have spoken up for you, for both of us, but I didn't."

"Oh, you were just a little boy. You shouldn't have had to choose between your sister and your parents. No one should ever have to do that."

"Parent's shouldn't send their children away and not tell them why, I realize that now that I'm an adult."

"They never told you either—I didn't know. Just assumed it was because I didn't make the cut and you did. It doesn't matter now."

"Yes it does, that's what I came here to say. It all matters and most especially, you matter. I'm sorry and I love you. I needed to say that." Gustavia couldn't believe what she was hearing. It was a surreal moment yet the warmth that flooded through her was surprisingly welcome.

For the second time in an hour, she was in tears as she reached out to pull him close then clung sobbing into his shoulder. All the walls between them fell and he held on just as tightly.

"I can't really explain how it feels to always be on the outside, especially in my own family. Vivian was so rigid, unyielding. So cold. She never hugged me or held me. Not once. Never said she was proud of me for anything."

Hugging her again, his heart broke for her. "I'm sorry," he repeated. "I'm here, now—for what it's worth—and I hope someday you can forgive me."

"I hope you can forgive me."

"For what?"

"For blaming you, envying you all these years. Thinking you were the reason I was sent away."

"Nothing to forgive. That was a natural response to the situation." Psych class with Professor Bainbridge had helped hone what he considered a natural instinct for understanding people's motivations. It made him a better cop and now, he hoped it would make him a better brother. His performance in the past hadn't been particularly stellar but if they could establish a firm footing today, he was sure their relationship would deepen. It was what he wanted and he hoped it was what she wanted also.

"Think we can make a new start?" He asked hopefully.

"Yes, of course we can. I'd really like that." She pulled him into the kitchen where he took a seat while she cleared up the remains of Finn's dinner. It felt right to have him there, comfortable.

"Good. Now tell me about Finn."

She rolled her eyes. "Nothing to tell. He's just..." She trailed off, it only took thinking of the man to make her blood pressure spike. Zack watched the play of emotions on her face. Oh, Finn's not the only one who's falling; she's got a case for him, too.

"I'll tell you what he is—he's a complication. One I should probably avoid."

Zack only nodded, from what he'd seen, avoidance wasn't her style. His sister, he proudly thought, was the type to face things head on. With no one to protect or stand for her, she'd had to become strong. Pride warred with shame for his part in it.

"He has a daughter. That's the biggest complication."

"Don't you like kids? I mean, you write books for

them. Makes sense you'd be, you know, kid friendly."

"No I love kids and I already love her. She's just this amazing girl. Spunky but sweet." She sighed. "Poor man lost his wife a couple years ago and he thinks the best way to protect his kid is by not bringing another woman into her life. Keep her from getting hurt again." Her tone revealed of a certain amount of skepticism.

"I see. And, you don't think that's an appropriate response?"

"I think it's an excuse. Not a flimsy one, mind you. I can understand his thinking and sympathize but I think he's protecting himself, not her. Otherwise, he would see how hungry she is to be around women."

"Complicated," he agreed.

"Didn't I say that? He pushes me away, makes ambiguous comments about my clothes, then calls me at night and we talk about stuff."

"Stuff?"

"Yeah, stuff. Nothing earth-shattering, we just talk and laugh. Then, when I let my defenses down, he does something crazy like kiss me then turn around and tell me he wishes he didn't. What kind of idiot man would say that right to a woman's face?"

Zack paused before answering what was probably a rhetorical question anyway. Blurting out his first thought—a man who is in love and isn't ready to admit it—wouldn't earn him any brother points.

He really needed those points.

"Sounds like he opens up on the phone because it gives him a sense of safety, anonymity even though he knows full well it's you on the other end of the conversation. Think past your emotions for a minute, what is your gut telling you about him? That he's a good guy or not?"

"Between you and me, I think he's a great guy but I think he's a scared camper." Zack frowned at her choice of words before making the connection— scared camper—happy camper? He let it pass. "Trouble is, every time he pulls the Jekyll and Hyde on me, it tugs on my own insecurities and leaves me feeling rejected. Again."

"Is he worth it?"

She sighed again. "Yeah, I think so. Not so sure he feels the same, though."

"Then, why does he keep calling?"

"I guess that's something to think about."

Changing topics, Zack validated Gustavia's instincts by confirming the Maverick's brake lines had been cut. He tried to cushion the blow by telling her his mechanic expected the repairs would only take a week or so.

The long day took its toll, her energy flagged. Zack noticed her increasing pallor and insisted on staying the night. Too used to being on her own, she would have refused, but one look at his set expression and she gave in, surprised at the unexpected feeling of safety washing over her.

It took three deep breaths before she began to feel less overwhelmed. I could get used to this, she thought. Feeling protected was a new experience, a good one. This brother-sister relationship could be promising.

After downing some painkillers, she showed him the little guest room and then let him bundle her off to bed. It had been one roller coaster of a day.

IN THE MORNING, Zack had taken delivery of her

loaner car, left the keys and a note but was gone by the time she got up so Gustavia tried to get back to her normal routine, have a quiet day.

The setting sun splashed the sky with orange shading through delicate pinks before deepening to purple as Gustavia typed feverishly on her laptop. The story was moving quickly now, so she'd buried herself in the work. At this rate, she was on track to finish well ahead of schedule.

Through the open patio door, she heard the chiming sound of her doorbell. Once, twice then three times. Whoever it was lacked patience. Out of habit, she hit the save button and went to answer the door. One look through the peephole and her heart sank. Standing on her front steps were the very last people in the world she wanted to see today. Her parents.

Closing her eyes for a moment as everything inside shot into battle mode, then, steeling herself for what was to come, she opened the door. Nothing good was likely to come of this. Nothing.

Nevertheless, she invited them in, offered them drinks and when they refused, got them seated.

"Eloise..." Her father started to speak.

"It's Gustavia," she interrupted firmly then watched the sour expression play across his face. "Eloise is a family name, one you should be proud to carry."

There was a time in her youth when she had been proud of the name. The idea that she was carrying on a family tradition had weight, made her feel special. After being sent away, the specialness was lost.

Here we go again, she thought, wonder which version of the you-don't-measure-up diatribe it will be tonight. He was about due for a new verse.

Gustavia began life as Eloise Roman, daughter of prosecutor turned Senator Peter Roman and cardiologist Dr. Janine Roman. For some obscure reason, one they never bothered to share, they'd sent her to live with Vivian, her grandmother on her father's side; a very proper and stern woman. Always disapproving, she'd made no effort to understand Eloise, treating her as an obligation.

Vivian's autocratic attempts to restrain her granddaughter's flamboyant nature had just the opposite effect causing clash after clash in their personalities. In her first year of college, Eloise Roman legally became Gustavia and used her childhood experiences to pen the first of a successful series of children's books featuring a mean old witch who mistreated her sweetly innocent granddaughter.

Janine shot her husband a quelling look which he chose to ignore completely. Given the chance, Janine would have come alone; she was ready to make amends and her ideas of how to bridge the cavernous gap between she and her daughter were very different from Peter's.

He continued to maintain that the family division had been a necessity while she was beginning to wonder exactly what could possibly have been behind the urgency.

Sending Eloise away had been necessary, not bringing her back had been Peter's idea, or maybe Vivian's she'd never been completely sure.

From one minute to the next, her family had been divided and for no good reason she could discern.

Month after month, year after year, the connection between she and her daughter had been through Vivian whose ever-present disapproval served as a wedge to drive the family even farther apart.

Vivian worked tirelessly to foster in Peter the opinion that Gustavia was little more than a wayward child. One, who could not be trusted, even as an adult, to take care of herself. News of her accident had scared him and his reaction to fear was always finding a way to exert control.

What he'd done—sending her away—had only been done to protect her. Why couldn't she see that?

Ignoring his wife's pointed stare, he continued on. "Gustavia," his use of her name sounded like a slur, "Zack told us you'd been in an accident, been hurt. Frankly, I'm disappointed in you."

"For having an accident? You are familiar with the concept, I assume. It wasn't planned. Or was it that I didn't successfully complete the accident to your satisfaction?"

How did the man manage to push her buttons so easily?

"Don't be ridiculous. You should have had the courtesy to inform us of the incident yourself."

Janine broke in. "We were concerned. Are you sure you weren't seriously injured? I could get you in to see one of my colleagues, run some tests. These provincial hospitals don't always have the latest equipment."

"I'm fine, Janine. Really." Gustavia made it a point to use her parent's given names; it helped maintain a certain amount of distance. Distance she needed for protection from even the prospect of closeness, she'd been burned too many times before. "It was just a little bump on the head. Your concern is touching, really." Her tone said the opposite.

"How long will it take you to pack your things? It's time you came home."

Mouth gaping like a landed fish, Gustavia was too shocked to answer. In a million years she couldn't have predicted those words coming out of his mouth. Her father looked at her expectantly.

When she didn't answer fast enough, his expression darkened.

Something in her snapped and she started to laugh. This was the funniest thing she'd heard in weeks. Before long, her eyes were brimming and she couldn't breathe. Finally, she began to get control until wiping the tears from her eyes, she caught a glimpse of the consternation on her father's face and it set her off again.

Her mother just sat there looking uncomfortable while her father, flushed with anger began to sputter.

Before he could get out whatever it was that he wanted to say, Gustavia's laughter abruptly subsided. "Don't say another word. I'm not a child to be ordered around and you gave up that right over thirteen years ago." She bit the words off angrily.

"Please..." Her mother began.

"Please what? Please co-operate? Please come home? I haven't had a home with you since I was a child, since I became too big an inconvenience and you sent me away. And, now, you walk into my home—the home, mind you, that you've never before deigned to set foot in—not in all the time I've owned it—and order me to pack. Dream on."

Janine had to try again. "We know we've made mistakes."

"Mistakes? You abandoned me, I can only assume,

because I didn't measure up to your standards. Didn't fall in line with your wishes. Didn't live my life according to your plan. Or was there some other reason? I wouldn't know since you never bothered to say, you just threw me away like trash. I was a child, just a child." She paused, her breath coming heavily as she finally spoke the words that showed her pain.

"Mistakes? Everything you did was deliberate and manipulative."

"Our intentions were..."

"Your intentions were paving the road to hell but I was the one who had to travel it." Gustavia's eyes fired then filled again, this time the tears were not from laughter. In a choked voice she said, "You sent me to her because I wasn't good enough for you. What kind of parents do that? What kind of people reject their own child? Let her be raised by someone who never hugged, never kissed, never approved of anything?"

"Is that what you really think happened?" Her mother asked in a hushed voice before her father spoke heatedly, "You will do as I ask or I will be forced to take action."

Peter spoke the words, reverted to his worst nature, the part of him Vivian had fostered when he knew he should comfort, tell her the truth. In that moment he hated himself and yet was powerless to change.

"And just what action could you take? I'm an adult, there's nothing more you can do to me."

His condescension grated her nerves. "We could freeze your trust fund."

Gustavia's laugh was not mirthful. "Go ahead, no skin off my nose. I've never touched a cent of your precious money." She could see by the widening of his eyes that he hadn't known that little tidbit of information. Obviously his money people hadn't kept him apprised.

"Is that the best you've got?" She paused, placing her hands on her hips and when he didn't speak, "You've got nothing."

She could see her father was winding up for another outburst but she didn't give him the chance to speak. "You need to leave. Now. Whatever you came here to do, it's over. I have a family here. People who care about me, people who love me like you never did." And with that, she went to the door and pointedly held it open.

As she moved past, Janine stopped, reached out a hand tentatively toward Gustavia's hair, then let it drop before softly saying, "Family is important." There were tears in her eyes as leaving those words echoing in her daughter's head, she passed through the door.

Family is important. Clearly, words the universe wanted Gustavia to hear. Firmly, she closed her ears and her mind to them. So tightly Estelle, who only wanted to help, to comfort, failed to make her presence known.

CHAPTER THIRTEEN

This time, when Gustavia showed up at Hayward House seeking solace and maybe a shoulder, Tyler very wisely took himself off for the evening. His grandfather could use the company and Gustavia needed female time, that much was clear.

Julie knew without asking there'd been a family related incident. As always, a confrontation with the Romans put Gustavia through a complex emotional ordeal; one painful to watch. This time, things were different, though. As she always did when these situations arose, Julie put on a pot of tea.

Settled with cups of steaming herbal goodness, Julie waited for the story and Gustavia spilled it in rapid fire bursts. Just the headlines.

"Zack showed up last night and get this, he apologized and he said he loved me. So that's the good. My car was sabotaged, that's the bad and then today, my parents came over, that's the ugly."

At Julie's nod, she continued, "Peter ordered me to get my things together, he wants me to move back home or else, and get this, he will cut off my trust fund money." Her eyes glittered with both anger and amusement. "He seemed surprised to learn that I wasn't drawing on the fund and none too happy when I found his threat highly amusing. I laughed in his face, then told him what's what and after that, I kicked the pair of them out my house."

"How did Janine react?"

"Truth be told, I didn't pay that much attention at the time, but now you ask, I think she really wanted to talk. As usual, he just kept cutting her off. You should have seen his face when I lowered the boom on him. Priceless."

Underneath the lighthearted tone, Julie saw uncertainty and a deeply seated wish that things were different. She changed the subject.

"And what happened with Finn taking you home? Anything interesting? I want details if they're juicy."

"He cooked, we talked, we laughed, it was good, then I cried, he kissed me, we fought and he left." It all came out in a rush.

"He kissed you."

"Figured you'd pick up on that part."

"And the kissing led to fighting?"

Gustavia inhaled, settling herself to tell the story.

"He kissed me then said he wished he hadn't. Not a very smooth technique."

"And he walked out without a limp?"

"Yeah. Guess I'm slipping."

Slipping, falling. Same thing as far as Julie could tell.

"That's when Zack showed up and we did the reconciliation thing before he gave me pain meds and sent me off to bed. He stayed in the guest room in case I needed him."

"That boy's heart is in the right place." Estelle spoke as she shimmered into visibility just before they heard the doorbell chime faintly.

"First the bell, then you appear, Grams." The sparkle in her eyes softened the dryness of Julie's tone. "It's what we agreed."

"I'm trying. I just can't seem to get the hang of it." An almost contrite Estelle said, then turning to Gustavia, "How are you feeling? Any headaches? Blurred vision?"

"You sound like my doctor. I'm fine, just a few sore places. I'm glad you're here. Did I see you and Julius right before the accident?"

"We put up a shield, tried to slow the car. It happened so fast, there wasn't much time but we did what we could."

"I'm grateful, can you tell Julius thank you for me?"

"Tell me yourself, though it's not necessary. It was that Logan wasn't it? He tampered with your car." Now Julius stood beside Estelle. "Been waiting for a chance to talk to the two of you alone. That boy's managed to shield himself strongly enough that I can't find him even when he's nearby. I think that's how he got past me to cut your brake lines."

A chill spilled over Gustavia. "Does that mean he knows about you? How could that be possible?"

"I think it might be worse. I'm getting the sense that there might be another spirit involved. You'd better get those men of yours digging into his history. Maybe he's getting a little extra help from this side of the curtain, same as you. Ask Kathleen, maybe she knows something." Then with a nod of his head to indicate he'd finished speaking his piece, Julius faded leaving the two women and Estelle alone again.

"Listen to him; he has more experience with being dead than I do. Now, back to what I was saying, your brother is a good man, Gustavia. He just needed some time and an adult perspective to see you as you are. That other one, the carpenter with the little girl, he's overwhelmed by fear. For her, for himself. He's fighting it but it's powerful and he's trying to turn you away with one hand while pulling you back with the other."

Gustavia nodded, Estelle nailed it, the situation was exactly as she said, push and pull. "What should I do? I don't want him if he's not in it fully. You know me, I don't do wishy-washy."

"He has to work it out on his own, you just be yourself. That's enough. For him and for everyone. Goes for those parents of yours, too." There was a speculative look in her eye. "Got a peek at your mother earlier."

Gustavia and Julie exchanged a meaningful look.

"No, I wasn't spying. I didn't go in the house, I was just making my rounds, I like to keep an eye on all of you, and happened to see them on their way out. Your father looked like someone shoved a skunk under his nose but your mother seemed genuinely upset," she mused.

"Maybe so. Not my problem." Gustavia was mutinous. She would not be pushed when it came to her family, not by Kat, not by Zack and not by Grams.

Estelle knew this was a touchy subject and she had her own opinions about the type of people who let such an amazing daughter feel so unloved, but sometimes a second chance was worth taking. Better not to push, though or she might do more harm than good.

"I'll leave you two to talk, then." She was gone.

"Busybody." Gustavia said but with affection.

"I heard that." Came a faint echo.

"I'll get Tyler on that research, see what he can find and if there are any blanks, we can get Zack to tug a few strings on his end so that part's easily sorted. What about the rest?"

"What rest? My parents? Nothing. It's up to them to make the moves."

"I meant Finn and you know it."

"Oh, him. I don't know. I knew he was running scared, maybe being a bit judgy but if it's that deep—well—that shines a different sun on things."

"Shines a different light?" Julie grinned.

"Whatever." Gustavia waved an impatient hand. "Way I see it, I can either sit back and leave it up to the universe or I can do something to help him."

Julie nodded in acknowledgment, "Any thoughts on what that might be?"

"Not yet, but I'll figure something out."

Julie pitied Finn. Just a bit.

AFTER HER conversation with Julie, Gustavia woke up feeling restless. She couldn't settle in to work so she spent some time tending her gardens. When that didn't relieve the feeling, she tried yoga, then meditation. She needed to do something. Something drastic. But what?

Things were changing, her relationship with Zack for one; whatever was going on with Finn for another. Julie would be getting married eventually. Another change. She'd taken a stand with her parents. Major change. It was time for more.

AN HOUR LATER, Gustavia strode into Bombshell, plunked herself down in the hairdresser's chair and ordered, "Cut it off. All of it."

Kalyn, the owner exchanged an uneasy glance with Sara the color expert and makeup artist.

"Do what now?"

"I don't know—give me a bob or a shag or whatever everyone else is having these days. I'm looking for a change; it's been too long since I did this. Go ultra-short, a nice pixie cut or something, I don't care, something crazy, something normal. Anything. As long as it's different."

Sighing at the lack of reaction, Gustavia began removing the clips and bands that secured her braids in place while Kalyn watched in trepidation. In her experience, when a customer asked for a total change they were in one of two head spaces. Happy and excited, ready for a new chapter in their life or hurting and angry. The former usually ended well while the latter rarely did.

In her professional estimation, Kalyn figured Gustavia was operating from a mix of the two or even from some third motivation, one the stylist couldn't quite pin down. "Darling, it's your hair, I'll cut it if you really want me to and it will be fabulous. I don't do normal and I can tell, you don't, either."

Six feet tall and willowy, Kalyn wore her own jet black hair in a severely angled, asymmetrical bob. Dramatic makeup drew attention to shrewd, ice-blue eyes; her lipstick was blood red. Simply dressed, she wore comfortable leggings under a billowy white blouse. This was a woman who would understand the need to project a certain image and stand out from the crowd.

"Listen. I used to change my look all the time. Short hair, long hair, dreads, every color of the rainbow. I like my braids, but people have come to expect me to look and dress a certain way. I put on a pair of jeans to do some work and all of a sudden I'm getting these shocked expressions and questions. Gets on my nerves."

Kalyn nodded in sympathy.

"My publicist wants me to tone it down so naturally, I ramp it up. Now, what used to be just me wearing clothes that make me happy, has become some kind of statement or something. People don't see me anymore, just the clothes and the hair."

"First impressions are always based on visual cues; it's what keeps me in business."

"Yeah, I get that. I know most people think I look like a whackadoo and I figure if they can't look past the outside—who needs them anyway? But now it has become a thing, you know? It's become expected and I hate doing the expected. Is that wrong?"

"Nah, its female. Unpredictable. We're built that way." Kalyn smiled.

Impatiently, Gustavia finished pulling out the braids then finger combed the thick mass. "Please?"

"You're sure?"

"It's only hair, it grows back. Just do it." Gustavia smiled.

Kalyn spun the chair and spoke to Gustavia's reflection as she lifted the thick mass, running her hands through its silky length.

"If we take off at least eight inches, you can donate

hair to make wigs for cancer patients." Kalyn's statement brought a beaming smile to Gustavia's face. "Oh, that's such a great idea. Please, yes, I want to do that."

"Do you want a drastic change just for the sake of it or something that will give you options? I'm thinking we could go shorter, say, a couple inches below shoulder length, layer it just a bit," she mused. "That leaves you enough to keep the braids when you want them. It will be versatile enough to let you play but still polished enough that you can do a quick blowout when you want something simpler."

"Do it. I'm in your hands."

Loosened, Gustavia's hair fell nearly to her waist.

"Okay. Here goes." Kalyn fitted an elastic band well above the minimum length for donation and asked, "Ready? Or maybe a glass of wine first?"

There was a nod, an intake of breath and then the sound of scissors snipping through the thick tail of hair.

Surprisingly, Gustavia felt no fear at all. She loved nothing more than bringing happiness to others and if she'd known donating hair was an option, she would have been on a mission to do it as often as possible.

"I'll take that wine now." Her smile brilliant, her eyes sparkling.

She surrendered herself to the feel of hands in her hair, the washing, the combing and the tug and pull accompanied by snipping sounds and the slithers of hair falling to the floor. She let Kalyn work her magic without direction, seemingly without interest. This moment signaled the outside manifestation of the changes in her life.

Somewhere between home and the salon, Gustavia

decided that getting a makeover was more than a response to the restlessness she'd experienced. Without realizing it, she'd slipped into a rut. Granted, it was a comfortable rut, she liked her clothes, liked dressing her outside in the colors and textures that best reflected her inner state. Still, sometimes it was tedious taking care of all that hair, and every so often the sound of bells and beads jingling and clanging together just flat got on her nerves.

Sometimes she wanted to wear black. Sometimes she just wanted to throw on something quick and simple, drag a comb through her hair and leave the house without confounding the image she had somehow created of herself.

Options, that's what Kalyn offered. That's exactly what she was looking for.

By the time she heard the blow dryer shut off, Gustavia had been lulled so deeply into a meditative state that Kalyn had to shake her shoulder to bring her out of it.

The woman in the mirror was a stranger. Beautiful, striking, but still a stranger. Just below shoulder length, the sleek mass of honey-colored hair was subtly layered to provide movement. She shook her head to see feather-like strands dance around her face then settle perfectly back into place.

"I like it. No, I love it. But, now the makeup looks wrong."

"Sara could do a makeover if you like."

"I only use organic stuff on my face." Gustavia cautioned.

"We carry a very good line of all natural products. Maybe a nice stress reducing facial to go along with your transformation? It's good for body and soul." Both women's kindness was like a soothing balm to Gustavia's jangled nerves. Nerves she'd just now begun to feel.

What had she done? Had she somehow sold out?

This was a major change, she thought as she took a deep breath and willed away the tension that was threatening to creep along her spine.

"Give me the works if you have time. I could use a little pampering." To Kalyn she said, "And I really do love the hair."

"Thanks." Kalyn was immensely relieved; angry, unhappy customers were bad for business.

An hour later, a very different looking Gustavia left the salon. Completely calm, she felt rejuvenated. With the weight of all that hair gone, her head felt strangely light. It had been a long while since she changed things up like this.

She was already picturing a new Gustavia-style hairdo. A bun on top with a corona of swizzle sticks.

NEXT STOP, that nice little boutique down the street. Finish the transformation some new clothes. The little store carried that new designer from the photo shoot from the day of the accident. She'd really liked those clothes. More mainstream than her current wardrobe but still bohemian enough to appeal to her free spirited sense of independence. Just the perfect balance.

Balance—just what she was striving for these days.

She was feeling fine as she pushed the door open, a tinkling bell announcing her presence but it was still several moments before a familiar looking older woman rounded the corner from the area at the back of the counter.

Gustavia's blood ran cold, then hot. Her mouth dropped open, held there for a moment before she remembered herself and snapped her jaws together. If she hadn't known better, she'd swear she was looking at her own grandmother. But that was impossible. Her grandmother wouldn't be caught dead on the other side of the counter in a retail establishment. Totally impossible.

It wasn't polite to stare but Gustavia couldn't seem to stop.

"What's the matter? Do I have something in my teeth?" The shopkeeper asked with smile. Her eyes crinkled at the corners indicating her smiles were frequent.

"No. It's just—I'm sorry. I was staring, it was rude. I really am sorry. You look like my grandmother. Exactly like her. It's uncanny." Her grandmother would never have smiled like that, either. So warm, so open. When Vivian smiled, it was with a self-satisfied expression. One mixed with a large quantity of condescension.

With a solemn look, the shopkeeper asked, "And, what is your grandmother's name?"

"Vivian Roman."

The older woman paled and Gustavia, afraid the woman might faint, didn't hesitate to move around the counter to provide an arm for support. Settling the older woman into a chair, Gustavia then knelt in front of her.

"What is it? Do you know my grandmother?"

Mouth working, the woman tried to speak but no words came.

"Can I get you some water?"

The woman shook her head. "No, no. I'm fine."

"Can you tell me? About Vivian?"

When the words came, they were none that Gustavia could have predicted.

"She's my sister."

Now Gustavia felt a bit lightheaded.

"So that makes you..."

"Great Aunt Valerie and you must be Peter's daughter?"

"I'm Gustavia."

"Now, I may not have been part of the family for many years, but I can't believe my sister would let any granddaughter of hers be named Gustavia." Her smile softened the words as Valerie twisted her hands, a sign of her inner turmoil.

"No, she didn't" It was Gustavia's turn to smile. "I was christened Eloise Roman, I changed it in college."

"Eloise was my grandmother's name. She was a wonderful woman, you have the look of her."

Gustavia's thoughts were racing. How on earth had she never known her grandmother had a sister? This was another betrayal in a long line of them. There was a story here, one she needed to learn.

"I'm sorry." She stood to pace the small area behind the counter, running her hands through her newly shortened hair. "They never—I never—I didn't know anything about you. Until this very minute, you understand? You didn't exist."

Valerie sighed. She'd expected nothing less from her sister.

All her life, Vivian followed a multitude of rules, real or imagined. Today, she would have been diagnosed with some form obsessive compulsive disorder but in her time she was just considered high strung. In her case, the disease went along with an autocratic personality which had Vivian convinced that in everything, her way was the correct way. Anyone who disagreed was summarily ignored or punished including their parents who had long since lost control of their eldest daughter.

A cold and unforgiving child, by the time she grew to be a young adult, Vivian was a nightmare. When Valerie, the younger sister married first, and to a man Vivian coveted, she'd turned her parent's life upside down until she convinced them to disown Valerie entirely.

From that day to this, Valerie had never seen her parents or sister again.

Vivian left her mark on every life she touched and Valerie didn't need a family history to figure out her sister had put some pretty deep emotional bruises on her own granddaughter. They showed. Her heart went out to the girl.

It was a lot to take in, for both of them. Finding family they'd never known; family with something in common. She stood, reached out toward Gustavia who, at first hesitated, then walked into the embrace and clung. Fresh tears coursing down both their faces, they embraced for long minutes.

Gustavia almost heard the little click as something, this one more thing, in her life slid into its proper place and for once, she didn't feel quite so alone.

Serendipity. Her restlessness completely eased, she was where the universe wanted her to be.

Chapter Fourteen

"We need a night out, something fun, something different. Gustavia could use a distraction. Suggestions?"

"Dancing. She loves to dance. We could take her to a club in the city," Amethyst suggested, then rethought the idea since mingling with the opposite sex was already partly to blame for Gustavia's current situation. "Or to be completely different, we could sign up for a class or something."

"Ooh, interesting. What kind of class? Not a painting or collage class, though, something we can all do."

"She likes to cook, there has to be a good cooking class we could take." Kat wouldn't mind honing her skills, either. Plus, it was fun to freak people out with her knife skills.

"That could work. What do you think? Some kind of fusion thing? Baking?" Julie was getting into the idea.

Amethyst fired up an app on her phone, did a search for classes that only lasted one night and read off the options.

"We've got an Italian, a Greek and a cake decorating with openings for tonight. All in the same building, but there are only 2 openings left in each class so we'll have to split up."

"Sign me up for Greek or Italian and Gustavia has always wanted to do cake decorating." Kat knew cake decorating was too visual for her abilities but either of the others should work just fine.

"Oh, I'll do Greek with you if Julie wants to decorate cakes with Gustavia." Amethyst was getting excited, this sounded like fun.

"Book it." Julie said, and she did; now they just had to spring the plan on Gustavia. "Any idea what the big surprise is? We talked for a while about her parent's surprise visit and about Finn yesterday. This morning, she texted me about some mysterious errand and a couple hours later, I got the request to meet her here, at her place."

"I got the same text so I finished up my last appointment, picked up Kat and came on over. Anything from the spooky side on the subject?"

Kat made a face at the reference but took no offense. "Nothing but I hear her loaner car coming up the block. It's got a little ping in the engine, very distinctive."

They all heard the slam of the car door and then Gustavia was coming through the door. She wore one of her new outfits and looked spectacular but different enough both Julie and Amethyst were speechless at first.

"What? What's going on?" Kat could sense something but was frustrated at not knowing what it was.

Excited, she twirled for effect. It wasn't until Kat

asked what was going on for the third time that Gustavia finally told her, "I got a makeover. Here, check out my new hair," and she pulled Kat to her feet to let her explore the new length and texture.

"A makeover? Because the old you was so last year." Kat's sarcasm was not intended to be hurtful, "Wow, you took off at least a foot, didn't you?"

"I donated it to the people who make wigs for cancer patients."

"Imagine my shock; you managed to turn your own makeover into an opportunity to help others." Amethyst broke into song, "Did you ever know that you're my hero." She sang with sincerity but also with tongue firmly planted in cheek.

Julie grinned from ear to ear. "You look amazing. Do you love it? Do you hate it? It's different but you still shine through."

"That's why I asked you to meet me here, I'm not sure what I think. I woke up feeling restless and had the idea, then I decided not to, then I went with the impulse and then reality set in and I freaked out a little."

Amethyst knew this was a significant moment, especially for someone who had been using her outward appearance to create certain perceptions in others. She could only think of two reasons Gustavia had chosen to make such a change. One of them was going to piss her off but she had to ask.

"Don't get me wrong, you look amazing, but did you do this because of Finn or your family? Or, did you do it for you?"

"See, you had to be here, you are the only one who would ask me the hard question; did I sell out?" She hugged Amethyst then stepped back, "Look at my aura, what do you see?"

"Mostly your normal colors but there's something different. Hmm...new color combinations and a lot less turbulence." She tilted her head and circled her friend several times. "It's not from the makeover, though. It's from something else. What happened?"

"Nail on the head, as usual. I don't know what I would do without you guys. It started out a rebellion against rebelling, if that makes any sense. I just wanted a change. It's so complicated."

She was finding it hard to explain but talking about it helped. Defining her choice for them also solidified it in her own mind.

"To answer your question, I did it for myself. If I've gotten to the place where my wearing a pair of jeans becomes a topic for conversation, something is wrong."

Pacing, she continued to work through her reasoning.

"I am Gustavia, whether my hair is long or short, in braids or not, whether I am wearing beads and bells or not, I am still the same person on the inside. Today, I choose to look like this. Tomorrow I might wear my hair in braids and dress the entire rainbow. I'm not even sure how or when I got locked into a single style. I like lots of different types of clothes and I like to play with my hair."

"Well, okay then. If it feels like the right reason, then all I can say is, dahling, you look stunning." She put on an accent and finished by kissing Gustavia on each cheek.

"I'm not throwing out my other clothes, just adding this stuff to my options and I plan on shopping more often. I already hit the craft store for a closeout sale on turkey feathers. I'm thinking they'd look good on a top.

Or, now that I have less hair, maybe I'll make a hat."

"Those clothes look familiar," Julie said.

"Yeah, from the designer from that photo shoot, found them in a little boutique near the salon."

Gustavia beamed. "My head feels so much lighter," she waggled a finger at Kat, "and no airhead jokes out of you, Miss Kathleen."

That got a grin out of Kat.

"Now, there's more. Something else happened today and if you think my new look is a bombshell, you've got to hear this," and she told them all about meeting Aunt Valerie finishing with, "Can you believe it?"

"Probably why your readings have shown you dealing with family. I have a sense that this is only the beginning. Things are better with your brother, now you have a new family member."

It was a blessing, Gustavia thought, having women friends who just get you.

Julie broke into the conversation. "We made some plans for a girl's night while we were waiting. What do you think about going into the city and taking a cooking class? You and I can do cake decorating and Ammie and Kat are hoping to master a new Greek dish."

"I'm in. When do we leave? Do we have time to stop for pizza on the way?"

He was late. He hated being late, it was a point of pride to be on time, to finish jobs on schedule, at least most of the time. Finn laid his tools out in the way he preferred. The panicked phone call that brought him here, hadn't left a lot of time, just enough to drop Sam at a friend's house for the evening and hightail it into

132

the city.

It wasn't the first time he'd bailed Lila's brother out and truth be told, he enjoyed the work. Building was building no matter what the medium.

There was only time for a quick walk around the room to make sure everything was ready before the doors opened and his students arrived. His welcoming smile froze when he saw Julie walk through the door talking animatedly with a woman who looked vaguely familiar. Catching sight of him, Julie's eyes widened in surprise causing her companion to look his way.

Whoa. That was Gustavia or was it? Wow—his gut tightened. She looked different. His heart skipped a beat; she always had that effect on him.

Could they have known he would be here? No, there was no way. He didn't know himself until the last minute when Toby's regular instructor had called in a panic; his wife had gone into labor several weeks early. It had to be a coincidence.

Realizing he'd been standing open-mouthed and mute for several seconds, he recovered his wits and welcomed his students. It was going to be an interesting evening.

"WELL, ISN'T that interesting?" Julie said quietly.

"You knew about this?" Gustavia accused, consternation and amusement battling it out inside.

"Not a clue." Gustavia arched her brows in disbelief. "No, I promise, total coincidence. We could leave if you want. Check out a club or something." Julie assured her.

Gustavia considered the choice. Amusement won. It

had been a crazy day, and if she could shake him up a bit, pure serendipity. Besides, Finn looked a little uncomfortable. It seemed they had discovered one of his secrets, so why not stick around and see what else they could learn. Hard to imagine him decorating cakes. Oh, the picture of him in an apron with the school name emblazoned across the bib, that was going to stick with her for days.

Or better yet, she pulled out her phone and snapped a quick shot. He did not look impressed.

On a quiet laugh, she lifted her chin and prepared to sail into battle.

"We'll stay," she said with a wicked grin, one that Julie had seen on any number of occasions and she almost felt sorry for Finn at that moment. Almost. The poor man was in for the full Gustavia experience. Oh yeah, Gustavia was back with a vengeance.

The cooking classroom had space for six teaching stations and a demonstration table for Finn to use. Each station was set up with a two layer cake, bowls of frosting, pastry bags, tips and spatulas, the sweet smell of sugar filled the room. Good thing men don't realize that if they only dabbed on a bit of frosting or chocolate instead of some of those stronger colognes, no woman could resist, Gustavia thought. Maybe frosting has pheromones in it.

Finn took his place and began by demonstrating the technique for establishing a smooth base layer to work from. Gustavia watched his hands, agile and strong, and only for a moment thought about how they might feel on her before pulling her attention back to his words.

He made it look easy and Gustavia had always considered herself a quick study so she was a bit surprised to find that imitating his actions did not produce a perfect result the first time. She dipped her spatula in the frosting and had another go at it. This time with a little more success, but when he'd made the rounds and ended up at her station, she leaned in close and let him guide her hand, quite satisfied at hearing the little intake of breath he couldn't quite mask when he touched her.

Keeping it simple, because at this point, he was having trouble concentrating on the lesson, Finn called the group to the front table and demonstrated how to pipe on a simple shell border around the bottom edge of the cake.

Julie watched with interest as Gustavia quickly mastered the motion then began to deliberately mess up. Before long, Finn was there, guiding her hand until she created a series of perfect shells. As he walked back toward the front, Gustavia glanced over at Julie and winked. Then, the next time Finn looked in her direction, she dipped her finger in the frosting and, with her eyes locked on his, tasted. Slowly, seductively, licking her finger clean.

He reddened slightly.

At each step, with each new skill: basket weave, leaves, ribbon and dot borders, they repeated the dance and the tension between them mounted as Julie watched. The poor man. Now she really did feel sorry for him.

Finally, the class was over and each participant had a boxed cake to take home. Gustavia signaled for Julie to go on ahead while she stayed behind for a moment. As the door closed behind her friend, she walked over to Finn, grabbed the front of his shirt and planted a hot one on him before he had time to think.

Then he couldn't think at all, could only feel. Her lips, warm on his, the sweet taste of sugar not quite able to cover the taste of her. The heady flavor that was hers alone. For a moment, they both rode the lightning, until she decided she was finished, pushed him away, and strode from the room.

Yeah, he thought, you can get her out of your system. Sure.

CHAPTER FIFTEEN

"You didn't?" Ammie nearly shrieked when Gustavia told the others about her after class encounter with Finn, then pulled out a ten and placed it in Kat's waiting hand. It was becoming such a common sight that no one even bothered to ask what the bet had been.

"I did. Say what you want, but the man's got a nice..."

"Butt?" Julie asked.

"Voice?" Kat chimed in.

"Shoulders?" Amethyst offered.

"Well, I was going to say set of lips, but that all works, too. He truly is very well put together."

"I really need to have Estelle lend me her eyes again." Kat muttered.

"Be worth it." Julie said. No one disagreed.

"His aura could use a bit of work, there are some dark spots and his heart colors are—I don't know quite how to describe it—pale and displaced." Amethyst waved her hands to indicate a spot near her heart. She was fishing for information and Gustavia knew it.

"Probably from losing his wife." Gustavia figured anyone who went through that type of ordeal would be burdened. "Lila's death put a lot on him, especially with the way Sam was struggling when I met them last year."

"He's the one," Kat said. "Your soul mate. It all fits." Gustavia rolled her eyes and Kat called her on it. How did she always know?

WHEN GUSTAVIA'S cell rang later that night and she saw Finn's name on the screen, she took a moment to decide whether or not to answer. She'd ridden the high generated by that kiss all the way home but with his history of flip-flopping on her, wariness seemed in order.

With a sigh, she clicked to answer the call. Best to meet the situation head on.

"What was that?" He was riled up. "And what did you do to yourself?"

"It's called a haircut. See, they have these places called salons where people with scissors style hair and other people pay them to do it. It's all very modern. Very convenient."

When the comment was met with a snort, she continued on, "I'm not sure whether you noticed, but I'm a woman, women often frequent these types of establishments."

"Oh, I noticed. Trust me, I noticed."

"Well, there you go, then. I'm glad we cleared that up. Is there anything else? Any other female convention I can explain for you?"

He changed the subject. "You kissed me."

"I did," she admitted.

"Why?"

Now it was her turn to snort. "Didn't you like it?"

She heard him breathe in and out loudly. His annoyance was easy to discern.

"Stupid question."

"Oh, I thought we were playing the stupid question game, you started it."

"Okay, then, here's one for you. Did you do it for me? Change the way you look because you were angry at me? Or because you thought I was judging you?"

And since that was a valid question, she answered it.

"Maybe—partly. But, mostly I did it for me. I should be able to cut my own hair without it being a momentous occasion and the fact that it has become such a big deal means I haven't been doing it nearly enough." As she made the comment, the truth of it sank in. "Don't flatter yourself. I'm not on the hunt or anything. You're safe."

Her words, the scorn behind them, added to his confusion and he snapped. "Safe. No one is safe. Lila was just driving to the grocery store. It was three miles away, a five minute drive, and now she's gone. Gone forever. Safe? Your car is in the shop right now because some creepy criminal type cut your brake lines and you almost..." He broke off then started right in again. "Safe. Please. No one is ever safe, no matter what you do. My daughter was slipping away from me and I couldn't do anything, couldn't keep her safe."

"Finn, I..."

"Don't talk to me about safe." Abruptly, he cut off the call.

Now she felt badly about upsetting him.

Chapter Sixteen

In order to write, Gustavia needed her ritual. First, she took a brisk walk around the neighborhood, just to get the blood moving. Next she set her phone to silent mode to reduce that distraction. Since it was summer, she carried her laptop out to the covered patio in her back yard. Rain or shine, the garden offered sights and sounds that boosted creativity. Then she burned some sage or incense to clear her head and finally, she meditated in order to contact her muse.

Today, none of her rituals were helping. It was payback for stirring Finn up last night. She'd been cruel in her own way. Lost in thought, she circled the block three times before noticing and no matter what she did, she just could not call her muse. Even the incense wouldn't burn. Every match she lit was quickly extinguished as though someone had blown it out.

Someone had.

Julius had been trying to get her attention and couldn't understand why she could neither see nor hear him when she'd easily done so in the past.

"Gypsy girl." He manifested himself as solidly as he could and called to her, again. He still couldn't bring himself to say the name Gustavia. "Gypsy Girl." Louder this time.

She lit another match, he blew it out. She stomped into the house and returned with a butane lighter. He blew it out. Three more times before her fogged thoughts cleared enough to realize something was strange.

Sinking into a deck chair, she called out, "I can't see you, but I know you're there."

"Gypsy girl." This time she heard him.

"Julius? What are you doing here? Is Julie okay?" Now, she could see him.

"Fine, fine. It's you I need to talk to." He was agitated.

Gustavia waited patiently for him to make his point.

"Family is important," he said, nodding his head emphatically, as though that one statement should make everything clear. It didn't. When she didn't respond, he shuffled his ghostly feet and repeated, "Family is important."

"You said that. Twice."

"Are you being deliberately obtuse?" He scowled.

"Are you being deliberately vague?" She countered.

"Family..."

"Don't say it. I heard you the first two times." Then it dawned on her. "Is this one of those cryptic clue things that you aren't allowed to say outright?"

That was it. She was sure of it when he didn't answer. Following that train of thought to its logical conclusion, she asked, "Are you talking about my family and does that have anything to do with the search for the second key?"

Nothing.

"I don't know why I asked but since you don't seem able to speak, I'll take that as a yes." A closer look at his face showed there was something more to be learned. It made no sense at all that her own family was directly involved so it must just be something to do with Julie's family. It was a clue. The first clue as far as she knew.

"Okay. Family is the first clue, something important about family. Am I right?"

Whatever had been holding him silent was released. "You know I can't confirm anything about the clue but Gypsy girl, you've got something stuck in your craw. It's to do with family and nothing can move forward until you make your peace. Estelle says your folks let you down badly."

Estelle had phrased it differently, much less diplomatically and with some name-calling, but it amounted to the same thing. Raising children without giving them a sense of safety, without loving them unconditionally—well—it was a crime in her book.

She shrugged and nodded.

"Just remember, not every family portrait is a pretty one." Julius stressed the words family portrait. "If you have a painful memory, you need to deal with it; you can't just lock it away." Emphasis on the last three words.

If that sounded like an odd thought, Gustavia put it down to his losing energy to speak and answered, "I'll remember," as he faded away.

His final words echoed back faintly, "You have the key."

Closing her laptop—writing today now seemed impossible—she texted the group, let them know about her experience. They had another clue.

GUSTAVIA ASKED Julie to invite everyone to Hayward House so she could tell the group about her visit from Julius. It was time they got serious about the next phase of the search.

The last one through the door, Gustavia was surprised to see Finn there with the others. Was he the Finn she laughed with on the phone or the one who had ranted and hung up on her? Hard to tell at a first glance. And they say women are moody. If gender was a prerequisite for moodiness, he was one man well acquainted with his feminine side.

Ignoring all that as well as the question of why he was there, she repeated Julius' words as he'd said them.

"What it boils down to is that we have the key, we only need to identify it and that it has something to do with family. Possibly a family portrait. I sense a trend. The last key was also a portrait," Tyler elaborated. "Julie, any family portraits in the house?"

"Assuming family portrait means a group rather than an individual, none that I can remember but maybe one will turn up."

"Well at least we're pretty sure the windows are part of the whole thing, right?" Kat said.

"Then we should go up and look at the rest of the windows." Gustavia said. "I don't think it's a coincidence that there are four of them, four seasons with their equinoxes and solstices and four hidden spaces. Maybe there will be something about the next window that will help us identify the key." Everyone followed Julie into the house and up the stairs.

"We found the first cache at summer solstice and the

next change of seasons is fall equinox. That would be September 23 this year. Sets the deadline for identifying and using the key." Gustavia spoke her thoughts aloud.

Amethyst picked up on her logic. "Fall equinox means we are probably looking for the window with the fall motif. Which one is that Julie?"

"It's in one of the closed off rooms." At one time, Julie's home had been a boarding home for war widows and their children. There were several bedrooms and baths on the second floor that now went unused. Partly because they were not needed and partly because of the money required for upkeep.

Before they'd found the first installment of the family fortune, she'd been considering ways to produce income and had thought of asking for a loan to turn the place into an inn or B&B. Now, they'd already scrubbed one suite down and turned it into an office workspace for Tyler and she was thinking of expanding her studio space. The rooms were still filled with period furniture that might work well for the fashion shoots she was now doing in increasing numbers. Repairs first, expansion later. She told herself.

JULIE LED THE way to the fall-themed window. It was just as spectacular as the summer one had been, depicting several large trees exploding in a riot of red, yellow and orange leaves against a vivid blue sky. The artist had used glass in varying degrees of opacity to fill out his color palette and cut the pieces to take advantage of the natural swirls created by the coloring process.

Each of the four windows was contained in a frame of richly colored oak elaborately carved with a branch and leaf motif matching the windows. Neither a visual inspection nor Kat's nimble fingers revealed a clue, there were no brackets to hold a painting in place as they had found on the summer themed window.

"Anything?" Gustavia queried when Kat had finished running her hands over the windows and the parts of the frame that she could reach. Reading braille made the blind psychic's fingertips exceptionally sensitive.

"Nothing on the frame, but I did feel something odd in the leading, here, here and here." She pointed to sections of leading that were not smooth and flat to the glass like the rest. These bits were curved outward to create a small lip. The anomalies were difficult to see but easy to find using her sense of touch.

Once she'd pointed them out, they found more. Ten in all.

Another clue. Or so they hoped.

Finn had remained quiet while Gustavia recounted her discussion with a ghost. He'd followed the others upstairs to look at the window, eager for a closer look at the workmanship. But, it was difficult to really wrap his head around this whole situation.

Could all of this be real? They'd found a hidden panel, he'd seen it for himself when Tyler had taken him to the library and pressed the button that operated the cleverly designed door. It was hard to be skeptical when you'd crawled into a treasure trove, even an empty one.

The idea of seeing a ghost was unnerving. In fact, his stomach was jumping at the thought.

Amused, Gustavia watched the emotions play across

his face. For once, he wasn't holding them back.

He stepped forward to make an observation.

"Notice how each of the areas with the leading anomalies is rounded?"

"What do you think it means?" Julie asked him.

"No clue," he glanced back at her. "Just an observation. It might come in handy later, every detail counts."

Amethyst said, "Must be a man thing, thinking about the details. Tyler has his lists." At that, everyone looked around to see him sitting on a chair, busily typing up an account of Gustavia's story and what they'd found by looking at the window.

Feeling all eyes on him, Tyler looked up, "What? I was just..."

"Making a list." It was a chorus of cheerful voices.

CHAPTER SEVENTEEN

"Good morning, young man. What's your name?" Finn hadn't heard anyone walking across the roof toward him. How had this older woman managed to sneak up on him like that?

"I'm Finn Kent, the roofing contractor." He held out a hand but with a funny, yet amused look on her face, the woman ignored the gesture.

"I'm Estelle, Julie's grandmother." I was right, Estelle thought, he does have enough sensitivity to see me, just like his daughter.

Remembering the story he'd heard at the cookout the other day, Finn paled under his tan. He'd just introduced himself to a ghost. "Umm hmm." He couldn't think of what to say next. In fact, he couldn't think at all.

Smiling as though she could read his thoughts, or lack of them, Estelle said, "I wanted to speak to you because I have a confession to make. I've spoken to your daughter, Samantha." She registered his shocked expression and the tension that immediately showed itself in the lines of his body, the set of his jaw, the spark of his eyes.

"I'm sorry, I can see this makes you angry and I

understand. I'd feel exactly the same way. In my defense, I didn't think she would be able to see me until it was too late and she already had. She's a lovely girl. Just beautiful. You should be proud of her, of yourself for the way you've raised her."

Emotions overwhelmed him. He was proud of Samantha, but she hadn't told him, hadn't said a word about seeing a ghost. It wasn't like her to keep something this big from him. Just having this sprung on him was disconcerting.

"Thank you for your honesty but I'm not sure where to go with this."

"I'm sure you know best. What I really wanted to talk to you about is my girl, Gustavia." As she spoke the words, she watched him even more closely. The tension ratcheted up even higher. Clearly, he had strong conflicting feelings.

"If I was a betting spirit, I'd put money on the fact she hasn't told you anything about her past. It's not my place to tell her story, though I will say it would be a mistake to make assumptions about her based on the surface. "

"I'm not that shallow." Anger flashed through him at the notion.

"Don't climb on your high horse with me, young man. I can see full well that you have some kind of feeling for her. Her history is complicated and painful. Do her the service of learning it," she said sternly.

"Yes, Ma'am." His mother raised him to be respectful of his elders.

Estelle winked out of sight leaving him feeling more conflicted than before.

"Something you want to tell me?" From across the dinner table, Finn pinned his daughter with an icy look. Uh-oh, she thought, busted.

"I had an interesting experience today, I met Estelle and she told me all about your little talk. Was there some reason you didn't tell me?"

"Are you mad at me?"

"Tell me your story. Then tell me why you didn't tell me before and then I'll figure out whether I'm mad not." He rubbed a hand over his face, took a deep breath then exhaled. He didn't look too freaked out, and when he reached over and took her hand, she knew it would be okay.

"Well, me and Lola went to the gazebo and we were playing princess. Lola was acting kinda funny, she kept looking at something, so I looked up and she just kind of appeared. Boy, did she seem surprised that I could see her. I think it was an accident. She asked me who I was and she was really super nice. When she told me she was a ghost, I wasn't scared. I asked about Mommy, to see if Estelle knew her, but she said Mommy would have been too sad to be a ghost and not be able to give hugs anymore so she probably went into the light."

Finn's heart felt like it was breaking all over again. He swallowed hard and concentrated on pulling back the tears that threatened to fill his eyes.

"Then she said that Mommy must have thought it was best to move on and leave a space for me to have another mommy, one who could give hugs and read me stories and kiss my cheeks."

Finn dropped his head into his hands. He had no idea she'd been thinking on these lines.

"I mean, really Dad, someday I'm going to need to learn how to put on makeup and stuff. Are you going to be able to show me how?"

Continuing to eat as though everything were still normal, Finn felt anything but. Sam had no idea her simple question had thrown his thoughts into turmoil. She needed a mother, wanted one. Was he protecting her from something that would give her happiness? At her next words, he put down his fork. The food had turned to dust in his mouth anyway.

"If I could pick a mommy, I know who it would be. I'd pick Miss Gustavia."

That got his attention but Sam had no idea the effect these words had on her father, she was too young to understand.

"The idea of a new mommy doesn't scare you?"

"No. Miss Gustavia isn't scary; she has warm hands and nice eyes. I know she gives the best hugs and I bet her kisses are nice, too."

Finn knew it was true.

"What if she had to leave like your other mommy?" Finn knew within a day of meeting her what a disservice it was to judge Gustavia by her outward appearance, he knew she was a loyal to a fault and he knew that anyone lucky enough to be loved by her would have that love forever. But, he had to ask the question anyway. If for no other reason than to gauge Sam's growth and recovery.

"Then I'd miss her but I'd be glad she was here for a little while. I know she wouldn't leave on purpose. She's too nice for that. Same as Mommy. Don't you think it was better to have had her for a little while than not to have her at all?"

Hugging his daughter, Finn wished he had her strength and her wisdom.

IT WAS less surprising to see Finn's name on the screen this time when he called.

"I have a coffee can full of rocks under my bed," he said when she answered. "One of those big commercial sized ones."

"I keep mine in the garden, that way people think they are part of the landscaping. They're all heart shaped."

"I have one that looks like Elvis." Gustavia slapped a hand over her mouth so he wouldn't hear her snort.

"I own the soundtrack to the musical episode of Buffy the Vampire Slayer." she admitted.

"My favorite episode." They laughed. It felt so comfortable, so right. Why couldn't they feel this way in person?

"My middle toe is longer than my big toe. Sam named it Stretch."

"I hear music whenever I use my blow dryer or vacuum cleaner. It used to make me think I was crazy but I looked it up and it's a thing. Common."

"I think Jello is weird. I mean, it wiggles. What's with that?"

"Caviar is worse. Looks more like eyes than eggs. Gives me the heebie jeebies."

"Well, people eat some strange things. Strangest thing I ever ate was one of those lollipops with a bug in the middle."

"A dare?"

"Drunk."

"Had to be one or the other."

They talked for over an hour, sharing confidences, embarrassing moments, little glimpses without judgment, without shame. The phone lent them both a feeling of anonymity that allowed him to open up without the fear that twisted him, turned him angry, surly. Bit by bit, they relaxed into each other.

"I'm getting sleepy," she finally admitted after stifling the third yawn.

"I'll hang up now, then."

"No, keep talking. Tell me about the worst house you ever worked on."

"Oh, that's not a story for the faint of heart."

"Guess it's a good thing I'm lionhearted, then." Pulling back the covers, Gustavia slid into bed, still holding the phone to her ear, listened to his voice rising and falling as she drifted off to sleep.

On the other end of the call, Finn heard her breathing slow and deepen. He knew she was asleep but continued to the end of his story then whispered, "Goodnight, sweet angel," before clicking the end button.

Chapter Eighteen

Sitting at her laptop, Gustavia was frustrated again, her mind clouded with non-writing thoughts that played havoc with her work. Words that used to flow and flood through her imagination and out her fingers now only came in fits and starts. She was just thinking she'd somehow managed to maim her muse when she heard the doorbell ring. Now what?

Distracted and not entirely sure she wanted to be bothered, Gustavia opened the door to find Julie standing on her front step looking like the cat who had swallowed the swallow. No, that wasn't right but it was some kind of bird. Maybe a parakeet.

"Did they find him? Is it over?" She asked as she tried to pull Julie into the room but was met with resistance.

"No, sorry. It's not that, it's just—I have a surprise for you. Just wait here, I'll be right back." She led Gustavia to a chair and practically pushed her into it. "No peeking." Julie went back outside.

Gustavia loved surprises.

Through the door she heard Julie's voice, then the door opened and a white ball of energy shot through and launched itself directly into her lap. The little dog wiggled twice then laid his head on the arm of the chair to gaze alertly into Gustavia's eyes.

"His name is Fritzie and he's a Jack Russell terrier." Gustavia ran her fingers through the uncharacteristically long fur with a frown. Fritzie had a much longer coat than was typical for the breed.

"He's adorable but you didn't tell me you were thinking of getting another dog."

"I'm not getting another dog. He's for you. Look at him. He's already in love with you."

It was true. One look was all it took to see that he'd immediately adopted Gustavia as his own. Julie's eyes filled with tears as she watched the bond forming. "Where did he come from? How did you find him?" Gustavia asked as Fritzie bounced in her lap and tried to swipe his little tongue over her face.

"Tyler's sister has an elderly neighbor who recently became ill and needed to move to an assisted living facility. She could have taken Fritzie with her, but he needs a bit more play than she can handle these days, so she was going to have to send him to the pound. When we heard the news, Tyler thought of you."

"So it's not payback for dropping Lola on you unannounced?"

"Oh, I didn't say that. Isn't serendipity one of your favorite words?" Julie's grin turned devilish. "But payback wasn't the primary reason, just a nice side benefit. This little guy needs a home and as a new dog owner, I can highly recommend the experience. Can he stay?"

"Yes, of course. I love him already."

"His things are in the car, I'll have Tyler bring them

in." She grinned. "He waited outside in case you said no. He didn't want to end up on your list if you had a negative reaction."

"Wimp." They spoke in unison, laughing over the shared thought.

Julie went to the door and gestured for Tyler to bring in Fritzie's things. He'd fallen for the dog himself and if Gustavia had refused, they'd have become a two-dog family. He had already made his mind up on that.

Putting the little dog down, Gustavia watched as he ran to the sliding glass patio doors and then looked at her pointedly. "Oh, I hope he's not a digger. My poor flower beds." But, she opened the door and they all followed him out into the back yard. He circled around once to get his bearings then made a beeline for the farthest corner where there was a small patch of taller grass and nothing planted. That was where he did his business.

"Polite little thing."

"Wish Lola was a bit more polite. She just bombs the yard wherever she happens to be." Tyler had been trying to train her to confine herself to a given area but had not been entirely successful unless he kept her on leash. He hoped she would eventually make the connection.

Changing the subject, Tyler asked, "Have you spoken to Zack lately?"

"Yes, he filled me in. I'll be careful and keep the security system on."

"See that you do." Tyler gave her a hug; she was one of his favorite people.

Julie suggested that Tyler give Fritzie a game of catch. She wanted to talk to Gustavia in private. It only took one lifted eyebrow for him to get the message and he grabbed a tennis ball and lobbed it for the dog who wiggled in ecstasy and raced for the catch.

"Can we go make a pot of tea?" Julie asked, then once in the kitchen, "You look tired." She tilted her head, "What's going on."

"I'm having trouble settling into the writing today. Well, again today. It's been a problem off and on since the showdown with Peter and Janine. Doesn't help that I've been staying up later at night."

"What's the protocol? Should I be dragging you off to visit Kat or Amethyst? Maybe both?"

Gustavia busied herself with the tea-making and Julie got the impression there was more to be learned. "Don't make me call Tyler in here, he's getting better at seeing auras and if he says yours is wonky or wrinkled or whatever, I'll take his word for it."

"I'll go see Amethyst if I need to. It's because he's been calling me."

"Who? Zack?"

"No, Finn. At night."

Aha, Julie thought. And there it is. "Is that becoming a problem for you? Did he turn into a breather?"

"No. Nothing like that." A genuine smile. "We just talk about random stuff. Like telling each other our most embarrassing moments or sharing secret vices. It's like he's this different person on the phone. We aren't openly flirting with each other, but there's some subtext."

"So, he's interested, wants to get to know you better, what's wrong with that?"

"It's putting me off balance and I don't like the feeling."

Yes, you do, Julie thought. You like it too much.

"I don't get it. On the phone, he can be charming, funny, engaging; but in person, he turns into an ogre half the time."

The word ogre sparked a few lines of story in her mind. Gustavia's eyes widened as she felt her whole body relax. "I think you just healed my aura or woke up my muse. Give me a minute." She grabbed a pad of paper and jotted down a few notes. When she lifted her head, it was to turn shining eyes toward Julie. "That's done it."

Gone was the pinched and hopeless look she'd had on her face when she had answered the door. Julie watched in delight as Gustavia got up to dance around the room, whooping and laughing. Once Tyler let him in, Fritzie joined his new owner, dancing and bouncing with joy.

Chapter Nineteen

Finally back in the groove, Gustavia wrote through the day and into the night. She caught up on the first draft of the new Ember book by adding a surly ogre with a split personality to the cast of characters.

Back on track with her work, that night's call from Finn was unable to alter her newly restored sense of balance.

In the morning, she breezed through another two chapters and then decided to take Fritzie over to meet Lola. Feeling especially light and airy, she chose every rainbow colored item of clothing she could find in her closet. When she left the house, she was wearing an eye-wateringly vivid skirt with a bull's eye tie-dyed pattern topped with an equally brilliant rainbow hued tank, rainbow flip flops and she'd woven her new, shorter braids around her head in a coronet formation with rainbow printed shoelaces hanging from them. The usual assortment of beads and bells complimented the outfit.

A quick text reassured her that Julie was free for the afternoon, so she loaded Fritzie into the car and drove on over. It had only been a day, but he was already fitting into her life as though he'd always been there. Happy to accompany her on her ritual pre-writing walks, his only demand was a game of fetch before he settled down at her feet while she typed. His absolute joy in the activity delighted her.

At this moment, life was good.

During the short drive, she talked to Fritzie about Lola. "Now, Lola is a big girl compared to you but she is very sweet so be on your best behavior. If the two of you get along, you can count on frequent doggy play dates since Jules and I spend a lot of time together." She thought he was listening, he was one smart cookie.

Gustavia pictured herself writing in the gazebo while the two dogs enjoyed time together. It was good to change it up sometimes.

Lola must have had her radar running hot because she was already gamboling toward the rental car before Gustavia brought it to a full stop. Tawny fur shining in the sun, tongue hanging out with a manic look in her eye, the boxer weighed in at nearly a hundred pounds. What she lacked in coordination she made up for in passion, running with abandon though not with any particular agility.

When she saw Fritzie jump out of the car, she detoured and practically ran right over him before she could stop. He yelped once and shot Gustavia a look that plainly asked what had just happened. Maybe they weren't destined to be best doggy buddies after all. But, when Lola had gotten herself stopped, she circled around and, little stump of a tail wagging like crazy, swiped her tongue across the top of Fritizie's head. He shivered once, then returned the favor and the two of them ran back the way Lola had come.

Figuring Julie or Tyler must be around back if Lola was outside, Gustavia didn't bother going in the house and instead, strolled across the lawn. She could see that the front side of the roof had been completely stripped, re-sheathed and was already dried in. She knew from her previous visit with Finn that the crew had already finished the two flat sections since those had been in the worst shape.

Rounding the corner, she saw she'd been correct in her assumption. Julie was in the back yard plying the roofing crew with her favorite beverage next to tea, fresh lemonade.

The men all stared as Gustavia came into view, and there were a couple of snickers until Finn's expression made it clear that he did not appreciate the attitude.

Even if the others thought she looked like a hot mess, Finn saw the joy. How could you not? It radiated off of her in waves. Julie watched the man watch Gustavia. Saw the play of emotions as attraction turned to apprehension and he tamped it down.

Doing a mental face palm, Julie knew that unless he found a way to let go, he was going to screw this up, royally. Hurt himself, hurt Gustavia and hurt his daughter in the process. Barely resisting the temptation to smack him on the back of the head, she poured a fresh glass of lemonade, greeting her friend with the refreshment.

"Looks like the dogs are getting along fine." She gestured to where they were playing tug a war with a fairly large stick, Lola clearly winning. "You've got to give him credit for trying."

Gustavia chuckled, "He is lionhearted, even in the face of incredible odds." Lola was about four times his size but he was holding his own.

"Your mood has improved a great deal since yesterday."

"The work is coming along nicely. I'm back on schedule."

"That's great news." Julie slung an arm around Gustavia's waist as they walked toward the gazebo leaving the men to finish their break on the patio.

Standing quietly while they walked away, Finn was still trying to fathom his own reaction to this woman. The sight of her nearly bare feet alone was enough to set a slow fire kindling in his blood. He pictured her dancing for him in that floaty skirt, the color whirling and whirling until his head spun and he felt all the tension falling away, felt himself falling into her. She was light, she was color, she was all. And what was she doing in his head anyway? He had to get her out, had to stop imagining those deep brown eyes staring into his as his lips lowered to hers. Stop imagining the silken texture of her hair, wavy from the braids as it brushed across his heated skin. She was a witch, which was the only explanation for how he could be both drawn to her and repelled at the same time.

Bands of fear tightened around his heart, strangling the words he wanted to say to her, the words he might forget himself and say to her from the safety of his phone but never in person.

With an effort, he shook off the mood and made his way over to the gazebo. He needed to talk to Julie, the weather report was calling for some much needed rain and he wanted to reassure her that they would be prepared. Of course, he didn't need to tell her at that exact moment, but he couldn't see any reason to wait.

Watching him walk toward them, neither woman could quite suppress an appreciative, "Mmmm." He was fine in every way with a rolling walk drew attention to his hips and how they moved. Pulling her thoughts away from that topic, she and Julie, reading each other's thoughts exchanged a quick grin. It was all Gustavia could do not to leer at him but she restrained herself.

As he got closer, the look on his face told her she'd made the right choice. This was not the easy, playful man she talked to late at night; this was the sneering jerk she'd met a couple times before. Julie saw neither of those men, she saw a scared little boy whose only way of connecting with girls was the childish act of hair pulling and poking. Sad really.

Finn did his best to avoid having to speak directly to Gustavia as he briefly told Julie about the expected weather and the steps he had taken to protect the roof from the rain. He turned back toward the house and almost managed to get away clean when Gustavia asked, "How's Samantha?"

"Fine, she's fine." He took another step.

"I'd be happy to hang out here for a day so she can come visit with Lola again."

He turned abruptly, his eyes firing. "That won't be necessary, thank you."

She responded by lifting an eyebrow. Clearly he had strong feelings about keeping her away from his daughter. .

Even after that searing kiss the other night, after endless conversations on the phone, he was back in rejection mode and this time, it flat ticked her off.

"Suit yourself," she said, her tone one of derisive amusement.

"Suit myself she says. As if I've been able to do that since the day I met her," he mumbled.

"Wake up on the wrong side of the world this morning did we?" Julie knew that tone, it was Gustavia's you've-hurt-my-feelings-so-I'm-going-to-be-nasty tone. Most people only saw the snark, Julie saw the pain behind it.

He strode away, his posture stiff.

"For what it's worth, I don't think it's you so much as his own personal demons." At Gustavia's fulminating look, Julie raised her hands in surrender. "Fine. I'll stay out of it if that's what you want. But, I stand by what I said, it's not you. Or not entirely anyway."

"It's enough me to be not entirely him and I don't know how that makes it not entirely me, entirely."

"Normally I'd say he did a number on you, but it looks to me like you're both the numberer and the numberee this time."

The comment earned Julie another disgusted look but she continued, "Way I see it, you can either wallow or turn warrior. Your choice. I love you either way. But, I'm going on record with thinking that underneath the attitude, Finn's a decent guy who's been through some stuff and has some scars. The kind that can paralyze."

"Not denying any of that, but the evidence doesn't lie. We talk on the phone for hours; he's charming, open and funny. In person, he acts like he has a cactus up his butt at the sight of me. So, I'm assuming his problem is just that—the sight of me, the way I look."

"Ugh. Thanks for the mental image."

"I don't want to be around people who judge based on superficial appearances."

"Everybody does it, though. Even you. Tell me you

didn't think I was one of those types the very first moment we met. I can admit I misjudged you at the outset."

Gustavia rolled her eyes. "For about a minute, but I take your point." She sighed.

"Here's the thing, you shine through. Not your hair, not your clothes, not your makeup, but you. The beauty of your soul, your Gustavia-ness, no matter what you have on. I saw it but it took me a minute or two because I was dazzled by your exterior. Why do you think kids fall for you? Because of the quirk? No, because they see what I saw. The light and the love."

"So you're telling me it doesn't matter what I wear? People are going to judge me whether I look like this or like Nancy Normal?"

"Have you looked in the mirror today? I think you're confusing normal with mundane. No. I'm telling you that some of those Nancy types who wear suits are wearing them for the same reasons you wear rainbows and shoelaces, for the protection and to project the image they think they should project. It's not you versus them and it shouldn't be. We all have to choose our armor one way or another. Sometimes mine is my camera. I can hide behind it and fade into the background."

"We women are complicated animals aren't we?"

Julie held up a hand, "Preaching to the choir."

"Confession time. I'm enjoying the options with the shorter hair. Now I can change it up and just wear my hair down when I want to, experiment with different styles, put on a mini or jeans and a simple top. Today, I felt like rainbows, tomorrow I might feel like something different, but I worry that people used to seeing me like this won't accept me any other way. Perverse isn't it?"

Julie pulled Gustavia in for a hug then held her at arm's length. "Screw that, screw them." She tilted her head appraisingly, "I say you wear what you want—what makes you happy. Anyone who can't see how wonderful you are—their loss."

Easier said than done.

A DUST COATED cobweb decorated Gustavia's hair as she backed out of the closet on her hands and knees. Three sneezes cleared her sinuses as she grinned at an equally filthy Julie. A tour of the unused rooms had netted them a new possible hiding place when they discovered several closets that had half-height cubbyholes in the back.

"Nothing but dust."

So far, their pile of booty consisted of three old shoes, a battered fedora that was now perched on Julie's head and a drawstring bag containing fourteen glass marbles. Not much of a haul and no family portraits in sight, but they still had two more closets to go.

A generation ago, the house had been used as a boarding home for war widows and their children. These women had banded together to support each other emotionally and financially by planting gardens on the spacious grounds. They called themselves the Weeping Widows. Gustavia fancied she could still feel their energy here in these rooms; their sorrow, their fear and eventually their hope.

They'd begun their search in the farthest areas of the house even though those were the least likely to yield results and now moved on to a set of rooms that had been used as storage to hold items cleared out to make space for the widows own belongings. If there was a missing portrait to find, this would probably be the place but it was also going to be the hardest to search. Full of cast-off and broken items, things Grams had planned on repairing and bits of machinery that Julius had cannibalized for his inventions, it was a total mess.

Julie opened the door and sighed. She already had a general idea of the contents since she and Tyler had made a pass through the room during their search last spring but they hadn't noticed those spaces in the closets last time.

There was a narrow path that got them halfway there before they had to start moving things away from the closet door. Half an hour of sweaty labor later, they managed to snake their way inside. The closet was full of vintage clothing, the kind that made Gustavia squeal in delight as she pawed through several items.

"Check out these dresses, authentic flapper wear. They're incredible," Gustavia exclaimed before ducking down and crawling toward the small space nestled into the eaves below.

No paintings, but she did find more old shoes and a whole box of hats to go with the dresses. Leaving the shoes alone and picking out a nice cloche hat, she passed the rest of the box back to Julie.

"Not much else in here. No—wait, there's another box here in the corner." She yanked and tugged. It was heavy but eventually she managed to pull it into the light where it promptly fell apart spilling its contents at Julie's feet.

Old photo albums.

They'd been so focused on finding a painting; they

hadn't considered the portrait might be a photograph. Each wearing her vintage hat, they maneuvered their way back through the maze of castoffs, carrying several albums.

Dumping their finds on the kitchen table, they washed up a bit then began to page through the books. Fifteen minutes later, they hit pay dirt. Toward the end of one of the albums they found a mounted vignette of a younger looking Julius with his parents, his wife and his new son.

Written in flowing script, the photo was labeled with the date and the words, family portrait.

They'd found they key. They hoped.

CHAPTER TWENTY

Kat laid out the cards, one at a time, in her favored Celtic spread.

First, for the question or significator card, she turned up the 2 of cups which had been a central card in most of Gustavia's readings over the past few months.

"New relationships or reconciliation. This card covers both meeting Valerie and your newfound peace with Zack. Your parents figure in here also."

The annoyed tone of Gustavia's sniff was unmistakable so Kat continued turning over the cards.

Second, the crossing card. Three of Swords. "Conflict but this card also implies a resolution to conflict. Clear away the past to start anew."

The next card she laid down, the crowning card was the page of cups.

"New love, renewed ability to love. This is really the theme of what's going on with you. Look what happened with Zack. That really fits here." Kat thought about avoiding the mention of Finn since it was a sore subject but went ahead anyway. "I mostly think it symbolizes Finn, though. His need to be open, your need for him to accept you."

Gustavia rolled her eyes. Kat knew but said nothing.

Fourth card, the one that shows the base of the problem, turned up. Justice.

"A sense of balance is going to be very important in resolving each of the conflicts indicated by the three of swords."

That got a sigh out of Gustavia. The emotional see saw she was on with Finn had affected her equilibrium.

"These past few weeks, I've been struggling with a lot of hard choices. I feel like I'm making steps, breaking out of the past. The makeover was part of that."

"And giving Finn a boot in the pants wasn't part of it?" Kat asked.

"Probably a little, but so was the need to explore my self-image and then, just for the not-at-all-fun of it, to see if it made a difference with my parents. Of course, I didn't think of that one until after I'd done it. The self-image thing is complicated."

Kat murmured her sympathy.

"I changed my mind three times on the way to the salon, I made a mental list of the pros and cons then wished I hadn't. Half the pros could have been cons and vice versa. By the time I got there, my brain felt like a cat chasing its tail. I never used to freak out over these things. It was nothing unusual for me to change hairstyles and colors three or four times a year, on a whim. Then at some point what I look like got all tangled up with what I am like and then that got hooked into my rejection issues and next thing you know I'm in a rut. A deep, deep rut."

"It's similar to how I use all my little tricks so people

aren't uncomfortable around my blindness. I sew a square button on the inside of all my blue clothing, a round one for red and so on, so I'm color coordinated. I fold each denomination of money differently to save time at the checkout and so I don't get ripped off. My blindness is the elephant in most rooms; people don't want to ask the questions that would make my life easier, mostly because they don't understand that they should. I get it, they don't want to offend or cause me pain but ignoring the situation just makes me feel marginalized. It's different for me because I was once sighted. I'm still able to relate to things based on how they look where someone blind from birth has no frame of reference."

"Oh, Kat, I hope I never make you feel that way." Gustavia's heart swelled with empathy.

"No, you don't. You always take the time to describe things with visual details. One of your greatest gifts is your ability to understand people and that you follow your instincts in the way you treat them. It comes from your own struggle for acceptance, I'm just sorry that this issue is coming back up for you."

"It's ridiculous how much effect something as simple as a haircut can have. Screw it. You know what's really ticking me off? A bunch of people never even noticed."

Kat had never heard her friend use that bitter tone before but Gustavia recognized it in herself. She'd spent years of her childhood dealing with the same feelings she'd been having lately. This was a blast from the past that she could easily live without.

Kat's mobile features took on a look of amusement which did not contribute positively to Gustavia's worsening mood.

"So, you figured out life's biggest secret. Most of the time, other people are struggling with their own inner demons and not even thinking about yours. None of us are as important as we seem to think."

With Gustavia's silence, the amusement fell away. "You're being too hard on yourself. What's wrong with wanting acceptance from your own family? With wanting them to be proud of you and feeling devastated when they aren't or if they are, they can't communicate it effectively. You're stuck with your past but you don't have to be stuck in it."

Kat chuckled in wry amusement. "Sage advice coming from me, I know. The hysterically blind leading the blind? Everything I've just said is something I have to work on, too. If I ever want to get my sight back."

It was nothing more than simple truth but somehow, acknowledging it as truth sent Gustavia in to a snit

"After the other night, reconciling with my folks is off the table." For one wild moment, seeing them on the other side of her door had sparked a flare of hope that things could be different. Sadly, the flare had died quickly enough under her father's controlling behavior. "It's all I've heard lately," she deepened her voice in a mockery of Julius' tone, "family is important." Then, she pitched it higher to imitate Kat herself. "You need to deal with your family".

She would have continued in that vein but was brought up short by the sight of Estelle's features settling over Kat's. It didn't matter how many times it happened, when Grams spoke through the psychic, the shift unnerved her.

"Gustavia." She recognized that tone having heard it once or twice before when she'd stepped out of line. It had its usual effect and stopped the tirade.

"I'm surprised at your tone. Being deliberately cruel is unlike you. Are you in so much pain that lashing out at others makes you feel better? Kathleen is only trying to help; she certainly does not deserve to be treated with so little consideration. It's truly shameful the way you've spoken to her."

"Yes, ma'am. I'm sorry."

"You don't owe me an apology but Kat certainly deserves one."

"I know. Can she hear me?"

"She can."

"Kat, I'm sorry. Truly."

"You're forgiven."

"Both of you?" The anger was gone as quickly as it had come leaving Gustavia feeling hollowed out from the force of it.

"Yes, dear girl. By both of us."

"It won't happen again." Gustavia, ashamed of her outburst, thought about the karma she'd just created and vowed to make it right. "Grams, what do you think I should do?"

Kat/Estelle considered the question.

"Your parents reached out, did they not? Clumsily, I'll admit, but they came to you with concern. I don't blame you for thinking it might be too little and too late. Aren't you curious to learn what prompted them to make the decision to send you to Vivian?"

"Oh, Grams. I've made a mess of things. I'm confused and I'm angry at the oddest moments, lately. First I thought Finn was judging me, then my parents showed up and I knew they were judging me, that's a given. Now I'm not so sure. I'm afraid my vision may have been clouded in both cases. A lot has happened over the past few weeks—I've met my great aunt Valerie."

Gustavia poured it all out quickly. Finn, her visit to the salon, then to the boutique and meeting her great aunt.

"Busy girl." The exasperated tone was softening but still there, the short sentence expressing a lack of sympathy. Gustavia squirmed a little. She knew the signs, Grams was about to lay down some wisdom.

"Has it occurred to you that Finn's actions might have more to do with him than with you? That they might not be personal?"

"He said that but..."

"And is it possible, just maybe, that your father was upset and concerned considering you'd been in an accident and he handled it badly? That all these years he's handled you, the situation, everything badly. After all, he was raised by the same cold and unforgiving woman that you lived with for several years."

"Well..."

"And maybe he isn't the only one? It takes two to have a conversation." She softened her tone. "I'm not making excuses for his decisions. I suspect his upbringing was in some ways as difficult as yours and that might be a factor in his relationship with you. Do you think Vivian treated him any differently than she treated her own sister, than she treated you? It must have been horrible growing up under that woman's thumb. Something you and your father have in common."

Surprised at the insight, Gustavia had never thought about her father's childhood before. She knew from experience that it must have been awful for him. Unexpected sympathy rose to take the place of impatience as she started to see him in a new way.

"Aunt Valerie told me about her life with my grandmother, it wasn't pretty. I've never thought about what his childhood might have been like." Gustavia sat down heavily in the dining room chair, eyes shining with unshed tears. "I've been so selfish."

"Nonsense, shortsighted maybe, but never selfish. It's a lot to take in and it's understandable that you might be struggling. I'm happy you've found your aunt." Kat/Estelle stroked Gustavia's hair. "Family is important."

"I know, I know. I've heard." A tremulous smile lit up Gustavia's face.

"By the way, you've always been beautiful, inside and out. New hair and clothes are just trappings. That's a matter of balance, too. How much does the way you look show your true self and how much does it distract people from seeing too deeply? It's a question all women face at some point." Estelle's features slid away from Kat's face like wax melting off a candle.

"It gets easier every time though I have to wonder why she does it when she could just show herself to you. She doesn't need me," Kat murmured.

Estelle had her reasons. Speaking through Kat was the best way to tell if she was progressing toward regaining her vision.

"Want the rest of that reading?"

"No, I guess I'm done for today." Gustavia had plenty to think about after her conversation with Estelle. Hugging Kat goodbye, she repeated her apology and went home to meditate for a while.

I T SEEMED as if work on the roof would never stop. The hammering and pounding was exciting yet not exactly conducive to a peaceful work environment. How Tyler managed to research and write through the noise was a mystery. Currently, he was knee deep in a collaborative project with his grandfather and enjoying every minute of it. Julie found the noise distracting.

Putting the finishing touches on the last of the images Gustavia had posed for, she was thankful for a different type of distraction when her cell beeped out the text tone.

My baby is fixed and I already turned in the loaner, can you give me a ride to the shop? —Gustavia

On it. Be there in twenty.—Julie

On the ride to the repair shop, Gustavia filled Julie in on her conversation with Estelle then they talked about Finn. "There's something there, for both of us, I think. I'm just not sure it's worth the effort."

"Okay, when did the world stop turning? You never give up on something you want. Why now? Why him?"

Gustavia had no answer or no good answer anyway. But, she'd always been honest with Julie so the lousy answer would have to do. "Reject him before he rejects me because he matters, already too much. Sam matters, too."

"Coward." Sometimes, Julie thought, you have to speak the hard truths and she'd do it for me.

"Come again?" Gustavia felt her heart sink. Of everyone in the world, Julie knew her best and those words from her were a blow.

"You heard me. I called you a coward. Reject him

first. Stupidest thing I've ever heard you say and that includes the time you tried to tell Grams we weren't drunk, we were seasick."

The memory drew a quick grin from Gustavia before she remembered she was both pissed off and hurt.

"He's running scared," Julie continued, "and so are you. For the same reasons. You were both abandoned by the people you loved. Maybe the circumstances were different but the outcome is the same."

"Okay, I guess I can see that."

"He's doing the same thing to you that you want to do to him. Rejecting you in some crazy attempt to keep himself from falling all the way, and then possibly losing you. You'd see it yourself if you weren't dealing with so many things at once."

"Now she makes with the insights."

"Maybe Kat rubbed off on me a little."

"Listen to her, she's making sense." Neither woman had noticed Estelle when she flickered into the back seat, now they both jumped and spoke at the same time.

"Warn a person."

"Geez, Grams."

"We really need to find a way to put a bell around her neck." Gustavia thought her heart rate might return to normal sometime this decade.

"Well, she is making sense but I believe we've already had this conversation."

Estelle was probably right; so was Julie, come to that. Not that she intended to admit it anytime soon. Besides, she wasn't falling for him and he sure wasn't falling for her so it was a moot point. Right?

"I just popped in to let you know that Julius got a glimmer from Logan earlier. He's nearby and I don't know if this makes him more or less dangerous, but he's very unsettled, scared."

"Yes," Julius chimed in making the two women jump again.

"I'm trying to drive, be easier if you two would quit scaring the life out of me every five minutes," Julie complained.

"Sorry." The two spoke from the back seat, neither sounding very sincere. Julius continued, "It was just a fleeting impression but it felt as though a cloud had lifted from his mind and for just a few moments, he had total clarity and it frightened him. Something has a firm grip on him, I thought it was just madness

but now, I'm not so sure."

"You said you thought he might be dealing with a negative spirit, could it have let go of him for a minute?"

"That's one explanation. Just wanted to let you know. Also wanted to tell you the photograph is not the key."

"Thanks," Gustavia said but they were already gone, leaving the women with several things to think about, not least of which was that if the photograph wasn't the key, they were back at square one. Julie felt a headache coming on.

CHAPTER TWENTY-ONE

Kicking her sneaker clad feet at the rungs of the dining room chair, Sam scrunched up her face.

It just wasn't fair. Daddy had let her go on job sites plenty of times. He even paid her for finding lost nails on the ground after the tear off process was over. She used this really cool magnet with wheels and every time she heard the metallic thunk of another nail being picked up, it meant a nickel in her pocket. But this time, when he was doing the best job in the world and she might get a chance to see Miss Gustavia, he always made her stay with Mrs. Millen.

How was she ever going to show Miss Gustavia how good a daughter she could be?

And Lola, she wanted to see Lola again. No, it really wasn't fair. If he didn't let her go with him tomorrow, she'd do something drastic.

While her father went into the kitchen for a drink, she quickly grabbed his cell phone and scrolled his contacts list to find Miss Gustavia's address. She knew that street; it wasn't far from Mrs. Millen's house. Only about five blocks.

"Bath time, Sam."

"Can I please go on the job tomorrow? You finished the tear off and now it's time for me to do the nail runs."

"Not this time. It's a big house and I wouldn't be able to keep an eye on you." Finn knew it was a flimsy excuse but it was all he had.

"I don't have to pick up nails, I could just hang out in the gazebo again with Lola." Her tone turned pleading. "Is Miss Gustavia there every day? Do you get to talk to her?"

"She comes and goes, but not every day." That much was true but his next answer was a total lie. "We don't talk when she is there, I don't think she likes me very much."

"Daddy, she has to like you if she is going to be my new mommy."

"Oh honey, that just isn't going to happen."

"Yes it is," She shouted. "She is going to be my mommy and you better not mess it up. She has to. It's what my first mommy wants. If she can't be with me, she wants me to have a mommy who can and she wouldn't want us to always be alone and you know it. She would want us to be happy, she wasn't mean like you." Sam stormed out of the room and a few moments later, Finn heard the sound of water splashing into the tub.

Her words cut him to the bone. Samantha was absolutely right. Lila wouldn't have left her family by choice and he knew without a sliver of doubt that his wife would kick his ass if she knew he'd let fear overwhelm him so badly that he wasn't listening to his heart.

The grocery store.

Just a short trip, not even a five minute drive. That's where Lila was going that day.

Preoccupied with the estimate he was working on, he'd barely kissed her goodbye. After they reconstructed the accident, police said the old man had suffered a heart attack right before he hit her car broadside. In the throes of his own death, his foot had jammed hard on the accelerator, causing the car to gain speed coming into the intersection. Just a freak moment in time and she was gone with no one left alive to blame.

After her bath, Sam's attitude had not improved, she was still sullen so Finn read her a short story and turned off the light.

In the morning, Sam didn't ask to go to Hayward House. When she came downstairs, he noticed she'd clumsily attempted to braid several toys into her hair. She didn't speak to him. This time her silence was accompanied by glowering stares which went ignored. He'd let it go because he was running late, but mostly because he had no idea how to handle the situation.

He missed his wife.

SNEAKING OUT of Mrs. Millen's house was easy. All she had to do was ask to walk to the corner market. Instead, she kept going until she found Miss Gustavia's house and rang the bell. When she heard barking from inside, she smiled with delight. Another dog to play with, this one sounded smaller than Lola.

Looking through the peephole, Gustavia saw Sam shifting from one foot to the other impatiently, her face a study of conflicting emotions.

About ten different options ran through Gustavia's mind in a blur. She should call Finn, there was no way he knew about this. She ran a hand through her hair, worn straight today, she was still getting used to the silky smooth texture after years of waves from braids. Keeping the girl waiting wasn't solving the problem so she opened the door.

"Miss Gustavia. You changed your hair, what happened to your braids?" Once she started talking, Sam couldn't seem to stop. "I—uh—I wanted to see you, so I walked over here from Mrs. Millen's house, she only lives five blocks away and it didn't take long."

"I can see that. Does anyone know you're here? Mrs. Millen? Your dad?"

"Well, no." Sam shuffled her feet. Maybe Miss Gustavia wasn't as cool as she thought. Not if she was going to rat her out first thing and that look on her face. Not very welcoming.

"We need to call them. If you've been missed, they're both going to be frantic."

"Are you angry with me?" Now Sam was worried.

"No, I'm not angry but I know your dad is going to be upset with me." She pulled out her phone and dreading his reaction, punched in Finn's number.

"Yeah," he answered abruptly.

"Finn, we have a situation here. Sam's come to visit me and it appears she left without Mrs. Millen's knowledge."

"I'll be right there and I'll call Mrs. Millen, let her know what happened." The headache hit him instantly, probably a result of the blood pressure spike her call had inspired. Sam's timing couldn't have been worse, the last person he wanted to see right now was

Gustavia. Seeing her was so much harder than talking to her on the phone.

Top priority? Get more male friends; there were entirely too many women in his life at the moment. Each one a bigger trial than the next.

"Okay, your dad's on the way. In the meantime, would you like to meet Fritzie?"

"Your dog? Oh, yes. I love dogs."

Gustavia opened the patio doors; she'd stashed Fritzie outside before answering the front door in case he rushed the little girl. He always became excited at the idea of meeting new people. Fritzie bolted inside but he wasn't alone, Estelle followed him into the room chuckling at the identical looks of surprise she received. From her favorite spot on the roof of the gazebo at Hayward House, she'd seen Finn stomp his way down the ladder and peel out of the driveway, face set in lines of anger and worry.

Because she could feel the waves of emotion rising from him, she'd peeked. His mind was awash with a mix of annoyance, uncertainty and sorrow all aimed at Gustavia.

"Young lady, what were you thinking?" Sam's head bowed in shame at Estelle's question. It finally occurred to her that she might have made a big mistake. All she wanted to do was see Miss Gustavia again, not stir up trouble. Tears of consternation began to slide down her face.

How was she ever going to deserve a new mommy if she kept getting into trouble?

"I just wanted to see Miss Gustavia and Daddy wouldn't take me to the job like he usually does. He's been all moody and it wasn't fair. I always get to work with him in the summer. Now I'm stuck with Mrs. Millen and she's nice enough but I wanted to see Lola and do the nail runs." Sam's voice rose with each sentence until she ended on a wail.

Unable to see anyone in pain without trying to help, Gustavia enfolded the miserable girl in a consoling hug and distracted her by asking how her dad ended up teaching cake decorating classes.

The ploy worked, Gustavia's question brought back Sam's smile as she explained that Finn considered cake art an exercise in architecture.

"But, don't tell anyone, he really does like to make whimsical cakes."

By the time they heard the slam of his truck door outside, everyone was calmer.

Telling Sam to stay with Fritzie, Gustavia hurried out the door, closing it behind her and met Finn as he was coming up the walkway. He was angry, furious in fact, and understandably so. Still, if they were going to fight, there was no need to do it in front of Sam. The girl was scared enough already.

"You don't want to intrude here, Gustavia. I'm not in the mood."

"I've no intention of getting in the middle of your family dynamic but I thought you should know exactly what it is that you are walking into."

"How did you get her to do this?" He didn't see the narrowing of her eyes, the steel that shot Gustavia's spine ramrod stiff and continued on. "Have you been speaking to her behind my back?" He would have continued moving toward the door but instead came up against a wall of very angry Gustavia when she stepped in front of him and drilled a finger into his chest.

It hurt.

"You've been exceptionally rude and I've let it go out of some misguided sense of sympathy but I've reached my limit. No, that's not true. I passed my limit with you already. I'm over it." He opened his mouth but before he could speak, she poked him again, hard enough that he took a step back. Where were the rainbows and sweetness now?

He opened his mouth to speak but before he could utter a word, she poked him a third time.

"I let you get me twisted, turned around. That stops now." His chest was getting sore from the poking.

"Your daughter came to me on her own. I haven't seen or spoken to her. You made it clear that you didn't appreciate my influence; that I wasn't good enough to spend time with her so I respected your wishes even when I could see that she is crying out for female attention."

She had him backed up nearly to the street now. "You don't have to like me. You don't have to respect me. Your choice, entirely. But, you will not come to my home and accuse me of corrupting your daughter. I saw the braids, I know that's next on your laundry list of complaints which, quite frankly, I don't want to hear so don't even start."

There was silence, while he continued to process the situation that brought him here. Chest heaving, she waited for him to say something. Instead, he pulled her to him and kissed the breath out of her. By the time he was done, she was pliant, melting in his arms. Then he let her go, strode to the door and went inside to deal with his daughter leaving Gustavia staring after him more confused than ever.

When she realized her mouth was hanging open, she shut it with a snap and refused to give in to the impulse to stomp her way into the house and repeat the kiss.

Crazy man.

Ten minutes later, Finn, accompanied by a grim-faced, very subdued Samantha walked out the door and made their way toward his truck.

Gustavia watched impassively, but did not approach the pair of them as Finn settled his daughter in the seat. He cast her one enigmatic look before driving away.

Oooh, that man. He got on her last nerve.

CHAPTER TWENTY-TWO

Torn between wanting to kiss him and wanting to kill him, which was where she'd been since the day she'd met Finn, Gustavia glared daggers at the trucks disappearing taillights.

Turning, she trudged into the house, hands balled into fists, teeth clenched, she took one look at Estelle who was still very much in evidence and chanted.

"I hate him, I hate him, I hate him."

Estelle said nothing, just looked at Gustavia with one eyebrow raised skeptically.

Then on a whisper, Gustavia finally admitted, "Oh Goddess, I think I might love him."

She felt it this time, when her aura went dark. It was all she could do to fire off a short text to Amethyst.

Hope you're free. Need you now. On my way —
Gustavia

Without waiting for a reply, without even resetting the house alarm, she drove out of town and up the hill to find comfort and healing.

ABJECT MISERY set in as Gustavia lurched into the pillows strewn across the meditation area. Hunched over, she huddled there, pain evident in her demeanor. Amethyst helplessly watched the other woman's aura as the normally bright colors swirled and seethed in a heavy, mud-colored mass half its usual size. She'd only seen this type of phenomenon a couple times before and knew that while she could provide guidance, it might not be in her power to intervene. Still, she would do what she could.

Kneeling beside Gustavia, Amethyst hesitantly reached into the teeming mass of darkness and began the process of flicking away the blackest spots. Usually this had the effect of replacing darker areas with light but this time the darkness was too dense. The blackness did not come away as it usually did and felt almost sticky in her hand. In fact, instead of being returned to the universe, the blackness began to expand and reach out for her.

Backing away, she now realized she was frightened. Something was deeply wrong. Something that might be a bigger problem than Gustavia's current mood. It was time to call in some help, she wasn't up to dealing with the situation on her own.

Amethyst grabbed her cell phone and called Mishka. "It's Gustavia, can you come?" Her voice was grave and Mishka quickly understood that something was terribly wrong.

"Ten minutes." Amethyst ended the call and began pulling the things she thought Mishka might need from her cupboards. Crystals, candles and sage to start. Amethyst, when pressed to describe her faith, considered herself a spiritual eclectic. Raised by church-going people, she'd always believed in a higher power but also felt that there was more, that one's faith should be inclusive, that there was something of the feminine missing from the picture. Seeing auras had not made her popular. At school or at church.

Everything as ready as she could make it, she reached for her phone again. Kat and Julie got the same text:

My house. Gustavia, code red.—Amethyst

Julie swung by Kat's place. On the way, they tried to prepare themselves for what a code red might involve. Whatever it was, they knew it couldn't be good.

Mishka slammed through the door several minutes later. She circled the prone woman several times before saying, "It's weighing on her. All of it. Her past, her family, whatever happened today, everything. I'm not sure what we can do to help if she's decided to wallow in the darkness. It's her choice, didn't know she was such a wimp, though."

Gustavia, deeply mired in self-pity heard these words and they did exactly what Mishka had hoped, they pissed her off.

"Don't talk about me like I'm not here. And don't call me a wimp."

"Well, what would you prefer? A wuss? A weeny? A coward?"

Gustavia came off the floor like a rocked. That last jab had hit her hard. "A coward? Is that what you think of me?" What had she done to deserve this? It was the second time someone had thrown that word at her.

"No, but it's your choice whether or not to spend time in the dark, feeling sorry for yourself."

"If I don't, who will?" Gustavia mumbled.

"You want pity? What's the point in that? We all have our stories but pity doesn't solve anything. Your parents get nasty or some guy doesn't fall at your feet and your solution is to go to the freaky dark side?"

It was working, her aura was lightening, colors returning, expanding. Amethyst glanced over at Mishka who, with a twinkle in her eye, turned her face away just enough so Gustavia wouldn't see and winked. Instead of a ritual of some kind, she'd recognized that anger and a good ass-kicking would burn away the fog and provide some clarity so she goaded her friend into a fine state of annoyance.

Annoyance didn't begin to cover it. Gustavia flashed right on past that stage and hit rage dead on. Face flushed, eyes firing like twin lasers she ranted. She paced, she stalked and she purged while Mishka and Amethyst watched and listened.

Kat and Julie came in about halfway through the litany, slid into seats as unobtrusively as possible and waited it out

Everything came out, the indifference of her parents, the fear and anger she felt while living with her grandmother. The never knowing why she'd been sent away. The struggle for acceptance that never came and the way the conflict with Finn brought it all back to the surface. The way he threw her off balance by appearing indifferent then kissing the breath out of her. It shouldn't be this complicated. Every time she spoke his name, she scrunched her nose in disgust or sighed like a lovesick teenager.

She talked about Zack and how great it felt that they were getting closer and how unexpected it had been to meet Valerie.

Eventually, she ran down like an overused battery, lapsing into a silence punctuated by a series of deep breaths. No more tears, no more angst as a cloak of quiet, calm peace settled over her.

Mishka was the first to speak her tone intentionally light-hearted if not slightly sarcastic, "Feel better now?"

"Matter of fact, I do." Gustavia slumped back down on the pillows, a wry smile on her face.

Watching, Amethyst thought she'd never seen an aura go through that type of transformation. Swirling darkness had gathered, swelled, and finally just drained out of her and into the earth as Gustavia released the anger, pain and fear.

The situation had not changed. She was still embroiled in several trying relationships, still in the cross hairs of a madman and still picking her way through the minefield of confronting an altering self-image. But none of that could touch her, Gustavia was back, centered and strong.

Goddess help Finn. And anyone else who got in her way.

HE CALLED three times that night before she decided to answer and when she did, she didn't speak.

"Are you there? Never mind, I can hear you thinking," he spoke into the silence. "That's fine, I need to talk anyway so maybe it's best if you just listen."

Gustavia waited, full of curiosity to hear what he had to say.

"I'm sorry. I know it wasn't your doing—Sam running away. I blew up before I had all the facts and dumped my family junk all over you. It wasn't fair. It took me by surprise. Not the idea my daughter might need something more than I can give her, I've always known that. But that she would search for more on her own like that."

Gustavia moved the phone from her left ear to her right. This was getting interesting.

He admitted, "Sam came to you because she knows you care for her. How do you do that? Love someone without being afraid? I watched it happen that first day when we had lunch. You just fell for her and that was it. No questioning, no worrying, just love. It's remarkable."

His words surprised her. Still, she waited.

"Are you still there? I hope you are." There was a pause, then he said, "True confession. I walked into a glass door at the mall once, knocked me right on my ass in front of everyone. I'm pretty sure my head bounced off it at least twice."

He assumed she'd forgiven him or he'd bared all of his soul that he could afford for one night. She let him off the hook.

"I'm addicted to the winter Olympics because it has become a necessity to watch curling at least once."

"Curling?" He repeated.

"It's fascinating. Kind of like shuffleboard for janitors. I make up stories about how it was invented."

"I tasted paste when I was in school. It was minty."

"I know, surprised me, too."

"Chickens hate me. I've been pecked more than once. I think they know I eat their kind. Not very manly, I know, but I avoid them."

"I'm scared of Guinea pigs. Not rats, not mice, not hamsters, just Guinea pigs." It was irrational, but their little faces creeped her out.

"Very specific. Is there a reason?"

"Not really, that's the weird part."

"I like talking to you."

"Figured, since you keep calling." She didn't want to talk about the why of it. That might ruin things.

"I watch chick flicks after Sam goes to bed." That one made her smile.

"Your favorite?"

"Nope, not telling."

"That ruins the whole true confessions game."

"Sorry. That information would require a major confession from you first."

She thought for a moment and decided to expose her deepest pain.

"I was an throwaway child."

That was one of the saddest things he'd ever heard. Now it was his turn to be silent as he thought about how lonely she must have been growing up. Her willingness to be vulnerable demanded the same from him.

"Lila was pregnant when she was killed. Sam doesn't know. No one did."

"Oh, Finn. I'm so sorry." Tears of sympathy filled her eyes as she understood how much deeper his loss had been.

"She was sure it was a boy this time. We were going to name him after my father. We were waiting until she passed her first trimester to share the news with our families. Once she was gone, I didn't want them to hurt more than they already were."

"So you carried this pain by yourself."

"I didn't know what else to do."

Her next statement shocked him. "Even though it comes from a good place, that's a very selfish thing you did."

"Excuse me." A chill in his voice.

"For two reasons. First, you didn't give your family the chance to grieve for your baby and second, you didn't let them support you and that would have helped them with their own grieving process."

Dead silence, she expected to hear the click as he hung up on her again, but it didn't come.

Finally, he spoke. "I never thought of it that way, just figured that by telling anyone, it would make it bigger. For them, for me, for Sam. I was drowning as it was, every breath like a knife in my heart."

"I get that and I wasn't judging. Asking for help, especially when you need it most, doesn't mean you're less, and it lets others become more. Hard to see that when you are in the middle, though."

"Speaking from experience?" The conversation felt balanced on a precipice, Gustavia thought her answer could push him away or put them on more solid ground. "My life hasn't been all kittens and rainbows. I know the darkness; I've lived the darkness. If not for Julie and Estelle—her Grams—I might still be in a dark place. I'd started to claw my way out but they took me in, loved me, healed me. Gave me the light without asking for anything from me. I owe them everything."

"She mentioned that." He mused.

"Who? Julie?"

"No, Estelle."

"You spoke to her? How? When?"

Now he was embarrassed, she could all but hear it over the phone. "She cornered me on the roof. Gave me a talking to, said she'd spoken to Sam. Then told me you had a story that I needed to hear."

It was her turn to go silent. "I told you my biggest secret, tell me what happened to you. What they did to you." At the gentleness in his voice, she came completely undone.

Hesitantly, she began, "When I was around the same age as Sam, my parents gave me away, sent me to live with my grandmother." Then, she told him the rest of the story. All of it. Telling him was different than her rant at Amethyst's house. That had been cathartic. This time, she was not angry or hurt; just resigned.

When she finished, he knew Estelle had been right to chastise him, he'd had some pretty well established ideas about her family life and background. Every one of them wrong.

And worse, he could see how his response to her, the one based on his own fear of getting too close, had caused her infinitely more pain than he'd known or intended. Worse, since he had yet to fully master that fear, instead of alleviating it, this epiphany fed the beast until it reared up swallowed him whole again.

Don't hurt her this time, he told himself when his first instinct was to push her away. Say something nice, something supportive. Nothing was coming to mind except panicked nonsense.

The silence dragged out until it became palpable between them. All the while, Finn tried to tame the flight response raging through him.

When he finally said, "I'm sorry," a slight inflection in his tone made the words sound like a question. He didn't hear it, though. All he heard was the buzzing in his head. Was that a lame thing to say? He meant it, he was sorry. For everything. Her experience and his own contribution.

Gustavia shook her head. Was he judging her again? Comparing his loss to her pain? She sighed. "This isn't a game where we trot out our worst memories for the world to judge, there's no prize if your past is more tragic than mine."

"No, I didn't mean...I meant...ah, that came out all wrong."

"Wrong or an unconscious slip that reveals a truth? It's not a competition to see if one of us is more damaged than the other."

"We're quite a pair."

"No, no we aren't. I hoped we might be a pair." She seemed to be thinking aloud, he wasn't sure she remembered he was still on the line. "In some ways we work. But it's too hard. It's all heat and sparks and shivers. Then it's a walk down memory lane at midnight on Halloween when every ghost from my past comes back to haunt me at once."

"I thought you love Estelle."

"Not her, it was a metaphor."

"Yeah, I got that, I was trying to lighten the mood."

"Consider it a fail."

"Lot of that going around since I met you," He helpfully pointed out.

What in the wide world did that mean? No, she was not going to get herself all twisted up again.

"I'm pretty sure Estelle was trying to tell you that I understand a little bit of what Sam felt when she lost Lila. Maybe our circumstances were different but I lost my mother, too."

"I really am sorry."

"I'm sorry you lost Lila, that Sam lost her mom."

At a loss for what to say next, all he could manage

was, "Goodnight Gustavia. Sweet dreams." He hung up, gently this time. The soft click sounded final.

"You, too," she said to the disconnected line.

Ah, what was she doing? Letting her guard down like that, telling him things she never meant to say out loud. And his goodnight had sounded like goodbye.

CHAPTER TWENTY-THREE

Finn watched from the shadowed booth at the back of the bar. He probably should never have allowed Sam to spend the night with a friend, after her performance the other day, she should still be grounded, but he'd needed the time alone. Time to clear his head a bit.

When the idea to stop in for a beer whispered into his mind, he never suspected Estelle might have planted it there. Not five minutes after settling into the back corner booth, he watched unbelieving of his bad timing, as Gustavia, Julie and the rest of the group trooped in and settled at one of the larger, center tables where they were joined by another woman who'd been waiting at the bar. With any luck, he could sneak out before one of them saw him.

Curiosity and the desire to finish his beer kept Finn sitting in the booth long enough to see the band greet all of them warmly and before there was time for them to even order drinks, all five women were pulled up to the stage. Unsure what was happening, Finn glanced around until he noticed a rather large sign he'd missed before. It was live Karaoke night.

All thought of sneaking away left his mind as he ordered another beer and waited to see what would happen next. Finn couldn't believe his eyes as Gustavia hugged the guitar player warmly before accepting the instrument and slinging the strap over her shoulder. Never once, during all their talks had she mentioned she had any musical talent. It struck him how little he actually knew of her, and how much he wanted to know more.

Julie took her place at the microphone and after a short discussion with the new arrival who picked up the bass, Kat took over the keyboard. Amethyst sat down behind the drums and slapped the sticks together three times before Gustavia flawlessly hit the opening notes to Satisfaction.

About two seconds in, he realized they were good. Julie's voice was silky but she still hit the sexy growl needed to sell the song. Gustavia played lead guitar the same way she did everything, with joy and abandon. It was the first time Finn had seen this side of her. Since the day they'd met, he'd only seen her through the lens of his own preconceptions.

Now, the real, the inner Gustavia again shone through and dazzled him. Tonight, her hair was braided again, woven with tiny rhinestones that caught the light and sparkled but even these paled in comparison to the brilliance of her smile, one that lit her eyes and clearly displayed the beauty within.

A warrior princess.

She had him. All of him. God, he hoped she wanted him.

With a sinking feeling, he figured it was probably too late.

S OMEONE WAS watching. Watching her, the group.

She'd felt it while they were playing, she felt it still.

Rebalanced and revving, Gustavia listened to her intuition. Trying not to draw attention to herself, she closed her eyes briefly, quieted her mind and opened up her awareness enough to home in on the watcher from the darkness.

There. There in the back, her senses pinpointed the source, the eyes intently focused on her. Without saying anything to anyone, she stood and stalked to the far corner of the room.

"The decent thing to do would be to just come and join us instead of skulking here by yourself," she told Finn.

Men weren't supposed to blush, he thought with embarrassment. How had she known he was watching and wishing he could join in? Chagrin turned him brusque.

"I can't sing. Thought it was better if I stayed out of it."

"No one asked you to sing. Come along now, and join in." A thought struck her and she took the seat across from him. "It's okay to enjoy a little fun; it doesn't take away from her memory. Finn, you still have to live and you have a right to a full life if you'd only let yourself. If she loved you the way I think she did, she would want you to move forward, be happy."

He ran a hand through his hair. Blame her insight, she'd picked up on his exact thoughts. Anguished eyes met hers and Gustavia knew she'd hit the target.

"It feels like a betrayal." He said simply.

"No, living a stunted life does not honor her. Tell me, honestly, what would she say if she could see you now, if she could come back for just one minute?"

Shrugging, he didn't answer but Gustavia knew she'd made her point.

"You're welcome to join us." She walked away.

Five minutes later, Finn grabbed his half-finished beer and made his way toward the group.

At one point, Gustavia watching him from the corner of her eye thought he was going to bolt. He stopped, started to turn back then squared his shoulders and moved forward.

Good for him, she thought, as she made room for him to join them. Instead, he set his drink on the table, and then pulled her to her feet, leading her toward the dance floor.

Well now was as good a time as any to see if he had the moves to keep up with her.

The song was upbeat and Gustavia cut loose. Krav Maga kept her fit but T'ai Chi made her graceful. She danced with abandon, totally enjoying the experience. Finn kept pace and when the song changed to something with a Latin flavor, pulled her into a fairly credible cha cha.

Another little surprise.

He could dance. He was almost the guy of her wishes. He had everything down except for being stable. His changing moods had him scoring low there. Gustavia sighed inwardly and wished he'd come around in that department.

FOR THEIR second number, Tyler joined the five

women and sang a duet with Julie that brought the house down. On the way back to their table, Julie stopped to talk to a couple seated nearby.

Tamara, a talkative redhead of indeterminate age, owned the jewelry store next door to the gallery where Julie displayed her work. It was Tamara who had pulled Julie first into doing product photography for her own line of jewelry, then into the world of fashion through a designer friend. Julie enjoyed the work and the doubled income was a nice bonus for doing something fun and artistic.

When Julie returned to their table, she saw that Zack Roman had joined the party. With an analytical eye, she watched him as he interacted with Gustavia. The siblings may have gotten past their differences, but Julie had yet to completely forgive him for his part in her friend's unhappiness. If he put one toe out of line, she was ready to stomp on it.

She needn't have worried. After a few minutes, Julie could see the easiness that now existed between the two of them. He'd even managed little more than a widening of the eyes when he'd caught sight of Mishka's pointed, elf-like ears peeking through her hair. Julie smiled and gave him points for trying. He was well on his way to earning a spot in their little family.

STANDING OUTSIDE the bar where he had followed Julie, Logan listened to the song. He couldn't believe she'd lowered herself to the level of singing in public. Good thing he was well shot of her but his blood still burned over the fact he hadn't completed his plan and gotten hold of her property. His big score and she'd foiled it. She and that crazy Gustavia. They needed to pay.

He strolled through the parking lot struggling with himself.

Something was wrong with him, he knew it. A good con man had to be willing to walk away when a mark got wise. Rule number one, never get emotional. Instead of being cold and logical, two personality traits he had ruthlessly adopted, he'd been overwhelmed by anger during the past few weeks. It made him sloppy. The screaming red descending inside his head until he couldn't think, couldn't reason things out and his entire being centered on revenge.

His daddy had taught him well, had taught him that when a con goes south, you have to know when to walk away.

He'd walked away but something kept bringing him back.

Worse, he didn't really remember coming back. He'd just suddenly find himself in Oakville with only a dreamlike picture of how or why he'd come. Hours, even days passed in a blur.

Logan stopped short when he saw the Maverick parked in a pool of light that spilled from one of the large streetlamps and slowly, the red crept over his mind again.

Hadn't he already taken care of her? Gotten rid of this hideous piece of junk? He couldn't restrain himself. Walking back to his car and grabbing a bat out of his trunk, he applied to her windshield, then to the headlights and rear window. He smashed every bit of glass he could find, each crash and tinkle feeding his fury until there was very little left of coherent thought.

All that remained was the need to break, to hurt, to annihilate. His last act was to grab the dancing hula gypsy doll, break it in half and throw it into the front seat before walking away. He hadn't covered more than a few yards before his memory of the act began to fade along with the red fury. He was back in his car and several blocks away when he heard the scream of sirens and wondered what had happened.

It was serendipitous, to use one of Gustavia's favorite words, that Tamara and her husband had just stepped into the parking lot when they heard the cracking of the bat and the sound of breaking glass. She whipped out her cell and called 9-1-1 while Logan was working over the windshield. Keeping her voice low so she wouldn't be heard and with her husband beside her, she crept silently toward the noise and reported the crime.

At first, in the dimly lit parking lot, she could only make out the movement, the glint off the metal baseball bat as it swung, but as her eyes adjusted, Tamara could see that it was Gustavia's car being assaulted. Knowing the story, her mind quickly jumped to identify the most likely person so she thumbed on her phone's camera, set it to the night setting and clicked off a few photos before Logan finished and strolled nonchalantly to his car. Doubtful the cops would be able to get a plate number, she fired off a shot of his car as it pulled out anyway.

The entire incident had only lasted a couple of minutes and now that it was over, Tamara became aware of her racing heart and shaking hands. She congratulated herself for being a quick thinker while her husband read her the riot act for getting too close to the action.

At the sound of approaching sirens, she left her husband to wait for the police and went inside to tell Gustavia and her friends what had happened. Since Zack was already there, she showed him the photos on her phone as he followed her out to the parking lot then became the second person to chastise her for taking a dangerous chance. Still, she could tell she'd made his job easier and he could tell by her cheerful grin that she wasn't the least bit repentant. She was thrilled to have helped.

This time, with Tamara's intervention, he might be able to get a roadblock in place quickly enough to catch the slippery slimeball. He made the calls to make it happen then escorted his sister over to take a look at the damage.

"Your insurance company isn't going to be happy about this." Zack tried to lighten the mood as he put an arm around Gustavia's shoulders and gave her a squeeze. Still unaccustomed to the easy affection he now displayed, she squeezed back.

"At least it was only the glass this time." Then she got a closer look, "Oh, and he killed Gertrude."

Zack's system went on alert until she explained that Gertrude was the gypsy doll and not a real person. Then, satisfied that he'd done his brotherly duty, he assigned a deputy to take Tamara's statement and left to make the rounds, cruise through town, check the roadblocks.

INSTEAD OF doing the smart thing and sneaking off into the night, Logan, his destructive activity now entirely forgotten, drove toward Julie's house. Bouts of rage eroding his thought processes to little more than instinct were coming more often now, the moments between them becoming less lucid every day.

Something inside kept driving him, even if he tried to fight it. Something that felt part of him, yet somehow alien.

Truth be told, he mostly embraced the feeling, the power of it was heady, enticing. Even when the voice told him to do something evil. Like now, it was telling him to burn it. Burn it all.

He parked the car and looked for something he could start a fire with. After his last experience of trying to break in here, he was loathe to run into Lola again and he could hear her barking from inside.

Wherever the voice in his head was coming from, it kept screaming, "Burn it. Burn it. Burn it down," until he couldn't hear anything else. Tearing through his car, he found nothing combustible, nothing that would burn strongly enough to set the house on fire.

Unable to satisfy the screaming voice, he picked up a rock and hurled it toward the house. It was just his bad luck that the rock broke a window, setting off the alarm.

The shrill noise pierced the veil and brought him back to himself. What was he doing here? This was a bad idea. He raced to his car, reversed and shot down the drive knowing full well that he had a very limited window of time to get away.

There was a turnoff a mile past the end of Julie's drive, if he could reach that, he could hide there until the cops went by, then get behind them and make his way out of town.

In the country darkness, he could hear the sirens getting closer as he rounded the last corner. It was a race he planned to win so he clicked off his headlights driving in the near darkness until he saw the turnoff ahead and reversed into it. It was going to be tricky timing his escape.

As soon as the flashing lights passed out of sight, he pulled out and hightailed it toward town. His luck held and he pulled into the municipal parking lot finding an empty space in a darkened corner. He reached in the back seat and rifled through the options there for disguise finally choosing a ball cap and a pair of heavy rimmed glasses.

Affecting an exaggerated limp, he took a seat at a recently vacated table in front of the pub, sat listening intently to the chatter around him. This was the best way to get Intel and before long he heard his name mentioned. They were saying he'd vandalized Gustavia's car and that there had been a road block set up on every road leaving town. They knew the make and model of the car he was driving so that was a complication.

Best thing to do was ditch the car and hide out until the heat died down.

Chapter Twenty-Four

Rubbing the sleep from her eyes, Gustavia reluctantly dragged herself out of bed. It had been a late night after the manhunt was finally called off. That Logan was one slippery character and once again, he'd managed to get away clean. Well, not quite clean, she amended. Thanks to Tamara, they had visible proof he had expanded his vendetta. Now, both she and Julie had to be careful.

Not that she'd needed confirmation but it didn't hurt to have it anyway.

When she walked into the living room, Zack was already up and working. It still felt weird to have him around but he'd insisted he wanted to stay, that she not be alone. Even with the alarm system, he wasn't taking any chances.

Smiling to herself, she listened to him muttering imprecations in a low-pitched voice while he alternatively chugged a cup of coffee and leafed through the files and folders spread out on her coffee table.

"Come here, take a look at this." He invited her to

sit. "I'm pretty sure this is how he got past us. There's an old access road for those camps down on the point, it used to be connected on both ends until the county took it over and they discontinued the lower end. It's not passable by car but hikers still use it."

"How did he find it? Never pegged him for being a hiker."

"Online aerial maps." He flipped his laptop around so she could see. "The forest hasn't fully reclaimed the old road so it's plainly visible from the air and the hikers have kept it clear enough to be an easy hike. Still, going through there at night shows he's desperate."

"How far away could he get on foot? Seems like you'd have picked him up by now."

"And so we would, but once he got past the blocks, he hitched a ride with an early morning delivery truck. Driver called it in after he saw the photo on the news."

"So, we're back to square one. Again."

"No, we have more evidence and now that his face is splashed all over the TV, it's only a matter of time."

Now he shifted uncomfortably in his seat. "There's more."

"What? Did he do more than vandalize my car?"

"No, I did something you probably won't like."

Remembering how little time had passed since he decided he cared what she might or might not like, she smiled. At his next words, the smile evaporated. "I called Mom and Dad."

"You did what?"

Just what she didn't need. More ultimatums, more awkward moments.

"Did you know he threatened to cut off my trust fund if I didn't pack up and go home with them? Does he think I'm still the child he threw away? Or that I would ever touch that money?"

"No, I didn't know, and don't look at me like that," he said as her expressively quirked eyebrow plainly said she didn't believe him. "Dad can be a bit heavy-handed at times. I assume you set him straight."

"Undoubtedly. He had no idea, all this time he thought I was living off his money. I take care of myself, always have."

"I'm not going to defend him—them. But I am going to ask you to keep an open mind. I know Mom wants a second chance. We've talked about you." She shot him another withering look. "I know, I know and I'm sorry. She's changed, she's softer. The past two years—I'm not sure what happened, but she's different. It's your choice, though, what to do about them."

Hands on her hips, she blew out a breath. "So you called them? And now what? Are they coming here? They're not coming here, right?"

The look on his face was all the answer she needed.

"When?"

He looked at his watch.

"You probably have a few minutes or so, enough time to get dressed."

"Thin ice, Roman. You're on very thin ice." She hadn't asked him about Valerie, hadn't asked if he'd known about his great aunt. If her parents were on the way, they needed to talk about how this family had a habit of throwing people away. She just wasn't sure where to start. "Can I ask you something?"

"Sure." The fierce expression made him feel a bit wary.

"Do you know about Valerie?"

"Valerie?" She could tell he'd drawn a total blank. Oh, God he didn't know. Well, at least she wasn't the only one for once.

"Vivian wasn't an only child. There was a younger sister, Valerie. I met her purely by accident, or fate stepped in depending on how you look at it."

At his stunned expression, she reached out, gave his hand a squeeze. "Vivian didn't care for the man Valerie married so she hounded her parents until they disowned her sister. Valerie was never allowed to associate with the family. I found her working in a clothes shop in the city. She looks just like Vivian except she has smile lines around her eyes and they're kind eyes, gentle. And why didn't we know about her?" She didn't realize she was crying until he brushed a tear from her cheek.

From the expression on his face, she could tell he was wondering the same thing.

"So what are you going to say to them when they get here?"

"You mean what are we going to say to them? You didn't think you were skipping out on this. Because you are staying right here, pal. This was your big idea. In fact, I ought to leave and let you handle them. They like you."

"I'll stay but you have to hear them out. Give them a chance. I know you don't think they deserve one and you might be right, I won't argue the point, but I'm asking you to be the bigger person."

"Is there more of that coffee? I need something stronger than tea this morning."

"There's half a pot left, but don't you think you ought to get dressed?" He turned back to his work and didn't see his sister make a series of sneering faces accompanied by several rude hand gestures before she went back to her room to pick out something to wear.

Because she needed to feel fully comfortable and firmly rooted in her own personality, she chose carefully. One of her favorite tie-dyed skirts, one of her new, more conservative tops. No scarves, minimal jewelry—only a couple strings of beads, rings on all fingers and toes—and then, just because she wanted to, she quickly wove ten thin braids into her hair then hung them with a series of oddly shaped, colored paper clips. Triangles and spirals mostly.

When she heard the doorbell ring, she raised her chin and prepared for the fight, the paper clips making a soft tingling sound that she imagined was the chain mail of her armor.

The three of them looked like a perfect family. Zack stood next to his mother, her hand on his arm, his head bowed low in order to listen attentively to what she had to say. Looking at the tableau, Gustavia knew she didn't fit and it didn't matter what she was wearing or how her hair was styled. Their differences went so much deeper and acceptance was scarce.

These people might, in their own way, care about her but none of them could understand the bone-deep loneliness that stemmed from not being included. From being deemed not good enough to keep, from being sent away.

No way was this a good idea, she thought. I'm just letting myself in for more pain. I can't do it. But, as she turned to escape back into her room, the jingling paper clips betrayed her presence.

Zack was instantly at her side, taking her arm and leading her closer to the family circle, one she knew was closed to her and would remain so.

Still, she had told Zack she would listen to what they had to say. So she waited for them to speak.

Her mother poked an elbow in her father's ribcage making him jump. Peter cleared his throat and opened his mouth to speak while his daughter waited expectantly. "I guess I owe you an apology," he said.

"Yes," she agreed and then Gustavia waited for the actual apology while he assumed his statement qualified as one.

He got another vicious poke in the ribs for his trouble. "I'm sorry. I was out of line the last time we spoke." It was not nearly enough but it was a start. Taking a deeper breath, Gustavia waited to see what would happen next.

Janine was overwhelmed with the need to touch her daughter. It had never been her idea for Eloise to live with Vivian but when her mother in law pushed, Peter had given in without a fight. At first, she'd thought Peter would come to his senses quickly, but it hadn't happened. Conditioned well, he always deferred to his overbearing mother.

He'd let his mother step in, make all the decisions and Janine had lost her daughter, maybe forever.

A logical woman at the top of her field, well respected and considered an authority, she'd allowed her own child to be taken from her without a fight. What did that say about her? What kind of mother refuses to fight for her family?

If Gustavia never spoke to her again, it would be no less than she deserved.

In despair, she knew she had to try. Stepping forward, Janine said, "You've cut your hair. It looks very nice."

A week ago, Janine's statement might have sent her daughter into another spiral of self-doubt and pity, but today, Gustavia only said, "Thank you."

Then, she fell silent again.

Now it was Janine's turn to search for words. "May we sit down? This might take some time."

"Of course, I'm sorry. Would you like something to drink? I could make tea or I have some fresh lemonade."

"Thank you, that would be lovely." Janine thought they all needed a moment to pull their thoughts together.

The moment Gustavia left the room, she turned toward Peter and in a low, but emphatic, voice informed him it was time to get everything out in the open and he'd tell his daughter the truth, or else. At that moment, anyone who knew both women would have seen an obvious resemblance between mother and daughter.

Finn would have recognized it right away as Janine drilled her finger into Peter's chest to make the point.

Well-deserved shame made Peter defensive; it was the trait his wife liked least about him.

Hearing the quiet slap of Gustavia's sandals on the polished hardwoods, Janine settled back into her seat and fixed a smile on her face as her daughter entered the room with a tray of drinks. It was a valiant smile but didn't quite mask the sorrow in her eyes; she deeply regretted the chasm in their relationship.

Gustavia faltered, just slightly, at the heightened level of emotion in the room. Coming from her mother. Zack might have been on to something with his idea that things had changed. Hope fluttered in her soul, wanted to break free and soar but she ruthlessly tamped it down again.

Burned me before, she thought, but it won't happen again.

Because she was watching carefully, Janine saw hope flare briefly and sent up a prayer that she could bring it back. If there was even a chance, she might just get her daughter back. Only if she could traverse the minefield of their past safely. Janine took a deep breath and plunged ahead.

"Sweetheart, we owe you an explanation. Are you willing to hear us out?"

Instinctively, Zack reached for his sister's hand, pulled her down to sit next to him. She would need his support.

After a moment, Gustavia nodded, her expressive face set in lines of defiance tinged with a fair amount of apprehension. Torn between wanting to hear the story and being afraid of what her father had to say, Gustavia lifted both hands, she scrubbed them across her face then squared her shoulders as if preparing to take a blow and said, "Go on, then."

Hesitantly, Peter began to speak. "I was still a prosecuting attorney when you were a little girl. There was a case—my biggest case—against a man well on his way to establishing a syndicate. He was a murderer and an extortionist with ties to drug and prostitution rings."

None of this was news to Gustavia. Did they think she was unaware of her own family history? That she'd never bothered to research her own father? Apparently so.

"The trial hadn't even started when a package came

to the door. It was full of pictures. Pictures of you playing outside, at school. Everywhere. There was no note but I got the idea. Unless I dropped the case, I couldn't be assured of your safety. When we started finding dead animals on the doorstep, we knew we had to do something."

Now that was new information.

"So you sent us to Vivian to keep us safe? How did you know they wouldn't find us there? It wasn't so far away."

"She hired a security firm at considerable expense; bodyguards, alarms, the works. The case dragged on for several months but we were able to keep our key witness protected and when the dust settled, we'd taken down the entire group. That was the case that propelled me into being elected."

A touch of conceit tinged his words, "I could have given in to the pressure but I followed through."

Peter would like to have ended his story there but Gustavia asked the key question, "When it was over, Zack went home but I stayed. Why was that?"

Now her father had the decency to look uncomfortable. "Mother thought it best," and when he didn't immediately elaborate, Gustavia turned to Janine with a questioning look.

"Wasn't it your place to decide what was best for me? Why couldn't the security firm protect us in our own home? Do you have any idea what living with her was like? Nothing you've said seems like a good enough reason to abandon me."

Peter cut in before Janine could answer.

"Mother insisted. She said you were too rebellious and that your outrageous behavior would be detrimental to my image, could hurt my campaign. We argued but I'm sorry to say that I didn't stand up to her." Peter at least had the decency to appear shamed at what seemed to Gustavia a flimsy excuse.

Until this moment, Zack had remained silent. Now, Gustavia was shocked to hear him ask, "Did you know about Valerie?" The question seemed to come out of nowhere.

"Valerie?" Peter seemed confused, "What does she have to do with anything? My aunt disgraced her family then ran away from home years and years ago."

"Did she?" Zack asked, "What did she do to disgrace her family? Marry a man who loved her and not Vivian?"

"She got pregnant, left home to become an unwed mother when she was sixteen."

"If that is what grandmother told you, she lied. I'm starting to think she lied about a lot of things."

When he got upset, Peter tended to resemble his mother, his face pinched and tight, his tone condescending. "Explain yourself," he ordered.

Zack bristled so Gustavia cut in. "Valerie was disowned by her parents after she married a man Vivian coveted. Vivian made their lives hell until they gave in to her demand and cut off a daughter who had done nothing to deserve it. Sound familiar?"

"How would you know anything about this, it all happened before I was born."

"Because I've met Valerie and she's told me her side of the story. It does not match what Vivian has told you."

Zack turned to Gustavia, "While you were getting dressed, I did a quick records search. The marriage certificate and her children's birth records are a matter of public record; easily accessible," Zack continued, his comments now directed to his father. "She had no reason to lie. Her first child was born a year and a half after her wedding; she was never an unwed mother. Never."

Peter's mouth worked but no sound emerged. Janine patted his hand thinking how difficult it must be to accept that his mother had deceived him. She wasn't surprised at all.

Gustavia sat back, stunned and happy that her brother was standing up against their grandmother. For the first time, she felt the wonder of having a family member on her side, it was a spectacular feeling.

"You've met her? How did that happen? Did she contact you? Maybe she's after something."

Shaking her head in disgust, Gustavia hoped her father would listen to reason, otherwise, she would consider him a lost cause, just like Vivian.

"I met her completely by accident, she was just as surprised as I was when we realized we were family, and before you ask, she's the spitting image of Vivian only with a much kinder face. I walked into a shop and there she was. It was a shock, I promise you."

"When Gustavia told me about her, I only had time for a quick records check, but her story holds. Considering she has never contacted anyone in the family, I doubt she's on the take." Gustavia rolled her eyes, Zack ignored her.

Looking from one to the other, Peter wondered how he would ever maintain control over his children if they banded together this way. That thought was followed by another. Why should he try to control them at all? They were adults and he was not his mother.

His mother. Peter still couldn't completely accept what she'd done.

Presenting his father with what he thought of as his "cop eye" Zack continued, "You didn't know the truth. I can't decide if that makes me feel better or worse."

Deeply flustered, Peter brushed the topic of Valerie aside. He'd come here, at the insistence of his wife, to make amends with his daughter. He had to make her see it hadn't been his fault.

"Mother said you were too wild for us to handle."

"I was nine years old, how wild could I be? At first it was my drawing that offended her. It was considered "unseemly" so she removed all of my art supplies from the house. I had to hide my favorite books or she would have taken those, too."

"So you admit to being rebellious? Hiding things from her."

Wild fury at anyone who condoned the hiding of books or the stifling of creativity shot through her like fire.

Standing now, Gustavia cried, "Did it never occur to you that I might have been rebelling against grandmother to get her to send me home? That I never felt safe or protected or loved? And you," she pointed to her mother, "don't you have anything to say?"

"I won't offer you excuses. There are none. Vivian made up her mind and we—I—didn't have the fortitude to stand up to her. I know living with her can't have been easy. She's not a warm person."

"Understatement of the century," Gustavia muttered. "She said you didn't want me and I was lucky she'd taken me on. That I didn't fit the wholesome image a senator's daughter should portray and it was necessary for you to distance yourself from anything that didn't "fit your station in life"."

"Is that why you dress like this and do the things you do? It only proves her point." Her father said.

Lifting her chin and standing tall, Gustavia replied, "No, I dress like this because despite being abandoned by my parents, I've managed to find happiness in my life, with my work and with my friends. I dress like this because the people who love me, who truly love me, will accept me for what is inside, not for how I look. And I dress like this because it makes me happy."

"So it's not a rebellion but a test? One we clearly failed." Janine was trying to understand. Whatever her husband said or did, she was determined to find a way to get her daughter back. Only now was she realizing just how much of an effect Vivian had had on Gustavia and how many broken places there were.

Weary of the conversation, Gustavia continued, "And just exactly which things did I do that you find unacceptable? I graduated with honors, am a successful author. I support myself nicely and have made a family with my friends. I'm happy, thank you for asking, with every area of my life that does not include dealing with you. If you've come here only to criticize and judge, you can leave." There was little anger behind the words now, just a sense of resignation.

Peter stood, intending to do as she asked. It was the final straw for Janine. "No. No. No." Each repetition of the word getting louder and more emphatic. She turned to her husband, "I will not walk away from my daughter again. If you choose to leave, you will do so without me." She turned to Gustavia, "I'm sorry. I know it's late in coming and the words are not nearly enough, but I mean it. I'm sorry."

I'm sorry, Gustavia thought. Not I love you, just I'm sorry. Those were nice words to hear even if they left her feeling cold, bruised and battered.

"Thank you." She said tonelessly, wrapping her arms around herself and hoping they would go before she started to cry.

Estelle, who had been watching the entire scene, had had enough. How could such an intelligent woman continue to be a complete dolt? Couldn't she see her daughter's pain, the need to hear those three little words? It wasn't the first time she'd wished for the chance to speak her mind, but at least this time she could do something. With a flick of her considerable will, she shielded her presence from sight and spoke directly to Janine sounding like the voice of conscience, "She needs to know you love her."

The words brought tears to her eyes and propelled Janine to her feet as she moved to Gustavia and enveloped her in a hug. "I love you. So much. Oh, I've missed you. Can you ever forgive me?"

At first Gustavia remained quiescent, it had been thirteen years since she'd been in her mother's arms. It felt warm and safe and familiar and alien all at the same time.

"Please, I love you so much." Janine repeated as she begged for forgiveness.

Now, Gustavia began to cry in earnest as she held on

tightly, her heart overflowing with emotion. Peter watched with envy. He wanted to be part of it all, he wanted to accept his daughter, be accepted by her, come to that, and recognized his reticence as part of Vivian's legacy.

Standing at a crossroads, Peter needed to choose between the cold aloofness he had always cultivated and the warmth and light that comes from being part of a loving family.

There might be consequences for meddling this way and she felt slightly guilty about doing it, but Estelle gave him a tiny mental nudge anyway. "You can choose to be like your mother or you can choose to love your daughter without limits. Don't be a fool."

With an inarticulate cry, Peter decided, launching himself toward his wife and daughter, his voice choked with emotion, "Oh, please, please forgive me. Let me be part of your life, let me love you," and was pulled into the embrace.

Zack watched with satisfaction before joining the group hug, his family was finally whole again.

CHAPTER TWENTY-FIVE

When Finn called that night, it was an exultant Gustavia who answered.

"Whoa," he said, "did you win the lottery or something?"

"Near enough. My parents—I think we are becoming a family again." She was overwhelmed with so many emotions. "We talked for hours. I can't remember when I've felt this good."

"I'm happy for you." She could hear the smile in his voice, the sincerity.

They talked for almost two hours. It was more than nice. It was a glimpse of what could be.

SHE'D GOTTEN her car, her baby, back for the second time. This time, when Zack's mechanic friend dropped her off, the Maverick had all new glass and Gustavia had even managed to repair Gertrude. If the Gypsy angel looked a little worse for the wear, Gustavia didn't care. Everyone had their scars, most would heal with time. This was something she was coming to understand as she placed the battered

Still, her heart beat sped up as she got closer to the address Valerie had given her. She was going to visit her aunt, the aunt who looked just like her grandmother. It was completely freaky; like one of those weird 3D pictures. The kind where you turn it just slightly and the image changes. Nice grandmotherly face then evil grandmotherly face. Gustavia shivered then shook it off. Valerie was a sweetheart and she was grateful for the chance to visit and get to know her aunt better.

Pulling into the drive she looked at the classic craftsman style home then took a moment to just sit, breathe and center herself. Wondering why she was so nervous, she was sure Valerie would be warm and welcoming. It was just all this "family is important" pressure. With an effort, she let it go and relaxed.

Nestled in one of the older neighborhoods, the house sat squarely in a pool of shade provided by towering maple trees. Potted plants and window boxes crowded with brightly blooming chrysanthemums gave a cheerful greeting.

Gustavia had barely stepped onto the porch, before the front door opened allowing Valerie to greet her warmly. All the tension melted away in the face of such welcome as she followed the older woman into the house. Gustavia looked around with interest; a person's decorating choices always said a lot about their personality. If her theory was correct, she and Valerie had plenty in common.

Just off the entrance, the living room, while not cluttered, contained a blend of highly polished antiques mixed in with a few quirkier pieces. Her aunt's taste in art was just as varied; Gustavia was especially drawn to one particular oil painting hanging over a gorgeous mahogany Georgian demi-lune table.

"That's an Estelle McLaren isn't it?" She asked.

"Yes. She was a lovely artist."

"And a lovely person. I knew her."

"I met her once a long time ago. We both attended a charity dinner and struck up a conversation. Such a warm personality but no nonsense at the same time." Her words raised a lump in Gustavia's throat.

"An apt description."

"When I saw this painting, it just spoke to me and I had to have it."

Gustavia knew the painting well. Against a lovely garden background, a young woman posed facing away, head bowed to show the graceful line of her neck, the side of her cheek where a single tear slid. Of course Gustavia knew the painting; it was her neck, her cheek so lovingly portrayed.

She turned to Valerie, eyes shining. "It's me, I posed for that painting. Did you know?"

At first, there was no answer. Gustavia turned to look searchingly at her great aunt who slowly shook her head. "No, I didn't know." The words were quiet, little more than a whisper.

Accepting the answer at its face value, Gustavia continued. "I spoke to my father. He had a very different story of why you were no longer part of the family. She lied to him. All these years she told him you'd left home in disgrace. Peter believed her."

"Of course he did, she is his mother, and he had no reason to doubt."

"That's all changed."

"Tell me about yourself, what do you do? Do you

have a family of your own?" Valerie changed the subject as though the past were too painful to deal with.

"I write children's books and I'm still single. I think I'm in a relationship or something that might become one. It's complicated." Explaining her current romantic situation would take more time than Gustavia wanted to spend. "Tell me about you, though, I'd like to hear about your family."

"The boutique where we met—it belongs to my daughter, I only work there once in a while. I also have a son. My husband died several years ago so I live here alone now."

They talked for several hours. Valerie pulled out photo albums from her own childhood, providing Gustavia with a deeper sense of her family history. Gustavia told her story, and it was a revelation to tell it all to someone who understood.

By unspoken mutual agreement, they skirted the topic of Vivian.

Finally, when Gustavia was just about to leave, Valerie said, "There's something I'd like you to have." Going over to a small hutch, she opened the top left drawer and pulled out a box which she presented to her niece.

With shaking hands, Gustavia opened the box to reveal a small, round, somewhat plain locket containing a photo of Valerie, Vivian and their parents.

"I had these made for my own children, it only seemed right that they have some memento of my side of the family. It took me a long time to come to a place where I could accept that they'd just let me go because it was easier than dealing with Vivian, but in the end, I needed to be rid of the animosity. For myself, not for them. So to commemorate my new found acceptance, we all got a family portrait locket."

Those words rang a bell inside Gustavia's head, one that echoed with Julius' voice. What was it he had said just before he'd faded away? "Not every family portrait is a pretty one," then something else and then, "you can't just lock it away." Family portrait locket. That was the key to Julie's next secret stash.

With an effort, Gustavia pulled her focus back to Valerie and thanking her for the gift, set a date to meet her new cousins. It was still a lot to take, this wealth of family after having so little. Gustavia was a bit overwhelmed by it all, though in a good way.

Before pulling out of the drive, Gustavia checked her brakes. It was a new habit, one she had adopted since the accident. Then, she drove straight to Hayward House and Julie.

SLAMMING THROUGH the door impatiently, Gustavia yelled out, "Jules, I've figured out the clue. I know what the key is." She did a little dance. "Jules, where are you?"

No answer, not even from Lola.

They probably couldn't hear her over the banging and shuffling noises coming from the workers on the roof. Eventually, Gustavia found the pair of them in the gazebo, Julie working on her laptop while Lola sat quietly at her owner's feet. Julie looked up as Gustavia bounded up the steps, her mouth quirking.

"Don't get me wrong, I'm glad the work is getting done and hey, the view from here is amazing at times, but these people are driving me crazy with the pounding."

Waving that away as a given, Gustavia burst out. "I figured it out. The key. I know what it is."

Julie's eyes widened. "And how did you do that?"

"Julius gave me the hint and then today, I was at Valerie's—Oh—hey, I was at Valerie's, she invited me—and she gave me a gift. A locket with a family portrait in it and I remembered how Julius kept harping about how family is important. Wasn't there a locket in with all the silver we found? One with a family picture inside? The locket, it's the key."

"Whoa, take a breath."

"That's it. I just know it. We have to call everyone, check it out."

FROM HIS vantage point on the roof, Finn watched the Maverick coast to a stop, watched as the swirl of a brightly colored skirt danced around nearly bare feet. She never looked up, never saw him there. If she had, Gustavia would have seen his true feelings; they were plastered all over his face.

The slamming of the back door sent a subtle vibration through the house, he felt it, even through sturdy work boots as he watched that spot of color make its way across the grass toward the gazebo. She was revving about something, he could tell by her posture, by the bounce of her step.

That million watt smile, even from this distance, it had the power to deliver a sucker punch to the gut.

If life were simple, he knew what he would do. Climb down off this roof, take her in his arms and never let her go. If life were simple.

But, it wasn't. Not simple. Fragile. He knew that better than anyone. How it could all change; how it could be ripped away when you least expect it.

Closing his eyes, he remembered how it felt to hold her close, to swallow the sigh of her breath, to feel her heart kick against his own. He wondered how he'd gotten sucked in, how she had managed to make it so that any day that went by without his seeing her or talking to her was empty and dull. Frowning, he decided she must be a witch and he was under her spell.

That was it; that was why he felt compelled to climb down the ladder and go to her. That thought made him furious. So furious he was already on the ground before he realized he had followed his thoughts with action.

She looked up as he stalked across the lawn, saw by the set lines of his body that he was in another of his moods, ready to push at her again. "Not this time, he's reached my limit," She spoke quietly to Julie and stood to face Finn.

Conviction a fire in his belly, he strode forward. Six feet or so from the gazebo, he stopped cold, his stomach dropping into his shoes. The look of cold fury on her face spoke more eloquently than any words she might have mustered. Drawing herself up to full height, she pointed behind him and said, "Turn around and walk away, Finn. Now. Whatever this was—the friendship, the more than friendship—it's over. Don't speak. Don't call me again. Just walk away."

Mouth agape, eyes wide, he watched her as she brushed past him and followed her own advice.

AMETHYST AND KAT both had clients so it was early evening before the group could assemble. Excitement was high as they waited while Julie fetched the locket from her jewelry box. She'd kept it for its sentimental value because in all fairness, as an adornment, it was much more to Gustavia's taste than her own. Large, chunky and ornate had never been her style.

Tarnished when she'd pulled it from the silver cache, Julie had polished the locket to a brilliant shine. It hung from

228

a thick chain formed from very tiny but intricately linked rings. The central face was round, decorated with a single oak leaf also wrought from silver. The leaf had been so skillfully created that each tiny vein was visible.

This center section snapped open to reveal a miniature family portrait protected behind a thin layer of glass. Then, on the rear, was a second latch that allowed the back to cleverly flip open then swivel downward to form a sort of stand. Julie supposed the idea had been for the piece to do double duty as a miniature frame or as jewelry. It was quite cleverly put together, in her opinion.

Around the upper half of the locket, on either side of the eye where the chain rode, there was a filigree formed from tiny silver hoops running down to the squared off bottom of its semi-circular shape.

They passed the locket around the room, from hand to hand, inspecting it closely in order to see if any of them could fathom its mystery. In the end, while each knew they'd found the key, not one of them could think of a way to use it with the window.

If Gustavia were right, they were one step closer to solving another of Julius' cryptic little clues. Not a big enough step, though, the equinox was only days away.

Chapter Twenty-Six

"Daddy, I heard you talking to someone last night, it sounded like you were talking to Miss Gustavia. How come it's okay for you to talk to her and I'm not allowed? Did she do something bad?"

He should have known she would see it that way.

"No, she didn't do anything bad. Miss Gustavia is a very nice person."

"You sounded happy, like when Mommy was alive." Sam's words were like a bucket of cold water, shocking Finn awake. More awake than he'd been in a long time. Sam sighed, "It was nice."

It had been nice and exciting and comfortable and warm and utterly terrifying. Talking to Gustavia made him feel all those things and more. And then he'd gone and blown it by turning chicken and trying to take it out on Gustavia. It was time to face up to his feelings for her and to Sam's.

"What would you think if I wanted to date Gustavia?"

"Would I get to see her sometimes?"

"Yeah, Junebug, you would. Dating me kind of

means dating you, too. If she's willing, that is. Does that scare you at all?" After today, he was probably getting Sam's hopes up for nothing, Gustavia had made it clear she was no longer interested in him. But still, he had to know.

"Why would I be scared of Miss Gustavia? She's one of my favorite people, the nicest person. Not scary at all."

"What if it didn't work out? I don't want you to get hurt." He thought he was telling the truth.

"Daddy." Placing her hands on her hips, Sam's tone was matter-of-fact. "When you taught me how to dive and I was scared, you told me to trust you and to just jump in and try."

He nodded.

"You said the only way to get better was to try and then learn from my mistakes and try again."

He could see where this was going and wondered how she had gotten so brave and so wise.

"If we date Miss Gustavia and someone makes a mistake, we can just learn from it and try again. I'd rather have her for a little while than not at all."

Was it really that simple? Maybe it was. Finally, the weight of fear lifted from him leaving his heart feeling lighter than it had in a long time.

"Okay Bug, let's give it a shot." Privately, he hoped he hadn't already blown it with Gustavia with his erratic behavior. A new fear settled over him but he was determined to make it right. Now he just needed to convince her he deserved a second or maybe, by now, he was up to a fifth chance.

AGAIN, IT WAS Kat whose sensitive fingers finally found the tiny catch, it was nothing more than a springy curl of thin wire, almost impossible to see, but when she prodded, the entire locket fell apart in her hand. She gasped and everyone leaned in to see that she now held ten thin rounds of colored glass. The pieces looked like lenses, each banded in silver with its finely-wrought wire hoop handle that when put back in place formed the decorative edging around the locket.

"Look everyone," she called out. "I think these might fit in those strange areas of the window. They feel as though they're about the right size."

Just that easily, they had the key and a general idea of how it worked. Only a couple of last details remained, finding the time of day to use the key and what order the colored lenses fit into the window. There were still three days to go before the equinox but that didn't stop them placing the lenses into the slots and trying out several color combinations. None yielded any worthwhile results so they sat around throwing out theories.

Weather reports called for rain on the day of the equinox and that was another cause for concern. The first key required the sun to strike the window at the right time of day. With no evidence to the contrary, it was assumed this key would work similarly.

Larger than an average locket, the portrait inside was still small enough that any clue it might hold was too small to see with the naked eye so Julie sent Tyler down to the studio to retrieve the loupe she used for inspecting grain in her photographs. Even with the magnifying device, she couldn't see anything within the photograph that yielded a clue to the correct time.

Maybe as long as the sun was shining, they would see whatever it was they needed to see.

If that were true, the only way to find out was to wait and hope the meteorologists were wrong.

"If we don't figure this out, we're going to end up sitting here all day staring at the window and wondering if we have the pieces in the right places. Maybe the time clue isn't in the photo. Let's have a look at the locket." Gustavia held out her hand impatiently. It took her almost no time to reassemble the pieces; she was incredibly good at building puzzles.

Once the locket was whole again, she turned it over and over in her hands looking for something, anything engraved into the silver. When she didn't find anything, she closed her eyes to connect more deeply with her intuition.

Grabbing the loupe, she inspected the patterns in the finely wrought leaf thinking there might be a number engraved into its lines. Nothing there either. Gustavia started to put the locket down when a new thought came to her. What if the leaf were meant to signify a clock. Becoming increasingly sure this was the case, she counted the spines on the leaf. Yes, there were twelve.

"Hey, guys? I think I'm onto something, here." Now that she could see the general outline of a clock, she just needed to find the hands or some other indicator of the time. "The oak leaf is a symbol, it's the clock." She passed the locket and magnifying device over to Tyler.

"Polishing it took away any residual imprint from the past." Amethyst said. "Kat, do you think you could pick anything up by holding it?"

"Probably not, I think whatever block keeps Julius from just telling us outright where to find each cache, keeps me from tuning in that way also."

Tyler took a quick look, passed the locket on to Julie and then opened his laptop to begin a search for any symbolic references to oak leaves. He found references to oak leaves being used in military insignia and in mythology but nothing that connected it with any particular number. He closed the laptop. "What if the time isn't on the locket? Maybe it's on the window."

Everyone trooped over to the window to look. Everyone but Gustavia who picked up the locket again. It's here, she thought. Not on the window but right here, I just need to figure it out. In the meantime, she admired the workmanship that had gone into crafting the piece. Each vein and texture faithfully wrought from silver; it had to have taken a fair amount of time. The silversmith had even added imperfections to the margins of the leaf.

A prickling feeling ran down her arms, raising the hairs. Gustavia grabbed the loupe again for a closer look. The tenth and fourth serrated spines were so skillfully crafted that the notches looked like naturally occurring damage but on closer inspection, she could see that each notch was in the shape of a tiny arrow.

"It's here, I've figured it out," and she told the others what she'd found.

"If Gustavia's theory is correct, we need to be in front of the window at either 10:20 am or 4:50 pm. That narrows it down nicely," Julie grinned.

"Not 4:50," Amethyst cut in, "this window faces toward the east, so it would get the strongest light in the morning."

Finally, things were coming together, they had a plan.

Finn dropped Sam off for a sleepover then tracked Gustavia down at Julie's house where the entire group had gathered. He had come to a decision and he needed to make things right with her.

The pre-Equinox party was in full swing with pizza, wine and a lighthearted atmosphere. The current plan was for everyone to stay the night and hope the weather would hold. Fritzie and Lola romped and played with a ratty old tennis ball.

When Julie answered the door, it was to a visibly tense Finn. "She here?" He asked without preliminary.

"Yeah, she's here." Julie might have been tempted to turn him away until he lifted his eyes and she saw the agony in them. Now, since she sympathized with him, she only cautioned, "Don't hurt her again." The "or else" was implied.

"I'm not planning to hurt her. Promise."

"Gustavia's very forgiving but even she has her limits. Best you can do is try."

"Okay." He nodded then took a deep breath and readied himself for what was to come. "Take me to her, please."

Julie led the way.

"Gustavia, there's someone here to see you." To the others she said, "Let's carry this mess to the kitchen and give them a chance to talk." Then she smiled as she saw Amethyst roll her eyes and pass yet another ten to Kat.

Unsure whether she wanted to hear what he had to say, Gustavia leveled an assessing stare at Finn, then deciding he looked properly contrite, she stood and waited for him to speak.

"I freaked out, I admit it. And I know there's no

excuse. I realize now my biggest crime was making you think I didn't appreciate everything you are. "

"Finn, I..."

She might have been a magnet, and he a piece of iron the way he was drawn closer to her. Close enough to touch.

"No, let me finish. I need to finish. I need to tell you." He brushed her cheek with the back of his hand, warm fingers absorbing the petal softness he found there. "You are perfect. Everything about you is honest and pure and good. Loves shines through you like the sun shines on the earth. And I can't believe I almost let you slip through my fingers." He took her cold hand in his and rested them both on his heart.

"Do you know when I fell for you? It was that first night we talked on the phone."

"You pushed me away, again and again."

"I was so busy projecting every bad thing that might happen that I couldn't accept the amazing good that had happened to me. I thought I was protecting Sam from getting hurt again, that if I somehow kept her from loving you, she would never have to try and heal from another loss."

"Finn."

"Shh. Let me. I need say it all and then if you want me to go, I'll leave. It wasn't Sam I was protecting, it was me. I thought that if I never loved anyone again, I would never have to risk losing that love. It was stupid. I was stupid; an idiot and I hurt you. Please let me love you. Please don't ask me to leave. I couldn't bear it if you did."

In that moment Gustavia couldn't speak, her throat was so tight with emotion that not even a whisper could pass her lips. Her eyes brimmed with unshed tears until she closed them, unable to bear the sight of his pain.

His heart sank in his chest. It was too late. She was going to close herself off from him, force him to live forever in the darkness of a life without her presence. He'd been a stubborn fool and he'd hurt her deeply. Too deeply for the wound to heal.

Gustavia thought about the wish she'd sent out into the universe. She'd asked for someone fun, stable, articulate, good with kids, nice body and he had to dance. Finn had scored on all counts except for stability but if he was determined to let go of his fear, she knew he was the one, her wish come true. Her frog was now her prince.

Then she opened her eyes and they shone with all of the love in her heart as she uttered one word.

"Stay."

The next second, she was in his arms, holding him and letting him hold her as he rained kisses across her face. Then he settled his mouth on hers, strong and sure, he poured everything into the kiss and Gustavia returned the favor. Mine, she thought, all mine. Forever.

As the kiss ended, they heard a loud whoop from the kitchen. Still holding her close, Finn quirked a brow in question. Gustavia grinned, face lighting up and said, "Well, you should probably know I come with an entourage and they all seem to have boundary issues." She raised her voice so the eavesdroppers could hear.

"I can handle it. As long as I have you, I can handle anything."

Unseen by choice, Estelle smiled through ghostly tears, now both her girls were loved.

In the middle of the night, crashing thunder woke the entire house. Finn, sleeping on the couch, woke in a panic, not quite sure where he was. After a few minutes, he heard voices in the room at the top of the stairs and followed his ears to the library where the others were gathering to discuss how the weather might complicate things.

After several minutes of futile speculation, Amethyst stated the obvious. "We need to talk to Julius. Would he come if we called him or do we need Kat? If she's willing, of course."

Kat spoke first, "I'll do it. It's probably the easiest way."

Finn wasn't sure what was going to happen next but he was interested and still slightly skeptical about what he might see. The process was much quieter and less dramatic than he expected.

Kat closed her eyes and concentrated for several minutes before anything happened. Then, her face shifted in that double exposure way as Julius features settled over hers. Finn shivered, it was uncanny.

Julius looked around the room with Kat's eyes. "Nice weather, eh?" he said.

"That's what we called you about. Will the key work if there's not enough sunlight?" Tyler asked. "Should there be some kind of contingency plan? Not that I know what one would possibly be, it's not like we can replicate the sun."

"I could, though." Julie said. "I have daylight balanced studio lighting; we could rig it up somehow, if we had to."

Kat's mouth open and closed several times as Julius

tried to speak but was prevented by whatever force it was that sometimes controlled him. Finally, he raised Kat's hands in surrender and his features slowly faded away.

As always, Gustavia's first thought was for Kat who was sometimes shaky after channeling spirit that way. This time, she was happy to see that Kat was suffering no ill after effects at all. She'd initiated the contact and was now used to the sensation. Used to having the ability to see, even briefly, it was no longer a shock to her system when her physical vision cleared. Gustavia hoped it meant she was also closer to regaining her sight, that her gift no longer generated enough fear to keep her blind.

"It's a good idea about the studio lights, there's still some staging here from the roof so access isn't too much of a problem and I can calculate the sun's position. If it doesn't work, then we wait until next year and hope for sun. Nothing more we can do now, I'm going back to bed." Tyler took charge.

Everyone else followed his lead.

Chapter Twenty-Seven

By 8:30 the next morning, the clouds were beginning to clear and it looked like the weather would cooperate. Finn, up before the rest, made himself comfortable in the kitchen. He liked to cook, it helped settle his nerves and after seeing Kat's stunning use of her abilities the night before, he discovered they were still a little jangly.

First a pot of coffee, then he decided to keep it simple. Pancakes were always a crowd pleaser and easy enough to mix together, even better with the addition of a few of the blueberries he found in the crisper. There was sausage and some veggie bacon so he added those to the menu and by the time everyone else stumbled in, breakfast was ready, everything kept warming in the oven.

"I could get used to this," Gustavia said as she greeted him with a quick kiss then put a kettle on for tea.

With breakfast over they all pitched in to clean up the kitchen then made their way to the window. Julie held the locket, it was almost time.

Estelle, as she had the last time they'd stood in front

of a window, key in hand, offered to provide Kat with sight. Grateful for the opportunity to watch and help, Kat agreed and opened her consciousness to allow Estelle easier access. When her vision cleared, Kat made a small sound of appreciation for the beauty of the stained glass window.

Finn watched closely as her eyes changed color then cleared. At the sight, a chill ran through him. On that first day, Tyler had warned him she was the real deal. All skepticism was now gone. No way to fake what he had just seen.

Stepping toward the window, Julie said, "We have ten glass lenses and there are ten slots in the leading, do we match them up by color? Like to like?" She waited for the others to chime in with their opinions.

Tyler opened his laptop and looked at the notes he'd made during their last experience with window and key. "I'd say we have around a ten minute window to figure it out. When we messed up the angle last time, it took a bit more than that before we realized something was wrong and the light had already moved."

They had less than half an hour left to brainstorm and in the end, they decided to place the lenses randomly. Hopefully, one would be in the correct placement and give them a clue to the rest.

Tension mounted as the minutes counted down. At 10:20, they were all watching as the light that had been slowly shifting began to stream though the lenses.

At first, there was nothing to see; until Amethyst, who had chosen to match a purple lens to a red space on the window, saw a blue letter form in her combination. "Look," She said, her deep voice rising in excitement, "red and purple works, there's a letter C in this one."

Kat was the next to find a letter when a yellow lens on a green window section also revealed a blue letter, an R.

"Match primary colors to the secondary ones, that's how it works." Gustavia and Julie both being artists, did the matching while the others recorded the letters as they came into view. T, A, I, E, V, H, another R, and then another A.

"It's another puzzle; how frustrating." Again, Amethyst stated the obvious.

"Sorry." Julius spoke from behind them. Finn whirled in surprise. Hard to get used to spirits flitting in and out of people and just showing up without warning. By the look on the spirit's face, he was anything but sorry. In fact, he looked fairly cheerful.

C-R-T-A-I-E-V-H-R-A

After a minute, they started throwing out guesses. "Something chair?" Amethyst said, "Or maybe heart something? I'm stumped."

Finn stepped back and looked at the window just as the effect faded and he knew. "It's the architrave," he all but shouted it.

"It's the what now?" Kat asked. It wasn't a word she heard every day.

"The architrave is that section above the columns in Greek architecture or it can be a type of lintel above a door." Gustavia explained. In his excitement and because he was happy that she knew the term, Finn grabbed her and gave her a smacking kiss. To the delight of all her friends, Gustavia blushed. They'd never let her live that down.

"How would we access it? From inside or outside?" Tyler wondered aloud.

"Depends on what's hidden, how the space was created and how the room behind it is laid out."

"We aren't sure what's hidden, but we have the house plans from the big remodel if that helps." Julie asked thankful Finn was now part of the group; he brought some skills to the table.

Frowning thoughtfully, Finn answered, "Maybe, but it doesn't make sense. The architrave is generally a solid, structural beam. I'm not sure how anyone would create a hiding place in a solid beam. But, as Gustavia pointed out, he might have meant the entire lintel area above the door."

"Always with the complications, Julius." Amethyst spoke to the spirit who promptly pasted a mutinous look on his face and replied, "Didn't want just anyone getting their hands on it, did I?"

A quick look at the plans yielded a bit of information, there was a space in the pediment above the architrave but they were no closer to figuring out how to access the area.

Finn and Tyler decided to set up some staging and take a closer look from the outside. Julie and her friends would inspect the corresponding area inside and hopefully, one of the groups would find the access. Julius flitted impatiently between both groups, visibly frustrated at his inability to provide any sort of guidance.

Because she had the best eye for that sort of thing, Gustavia was the one sent out to gauge the height of the architrave, they needed to estimate whether the most likely access point would be upstairs or downstairs.

"Upstairs," She pronounced. "Just about level with the floor, I think."

The four women made their way up to Estelle's old room, now Julie's, only to find a stretch of bare, blank wall in the spot Gustavia indicated. Amethyst swore and handed Kat a crisp five dollar bill then, fuming, stalked back downstairs and outside to see if the men had found anything while Julie and Gustavia exchanged a knowing eyebrow quirk then, along with Kat, followed her. At least she'd only lost five this time.

Judging by the dark looks on their faces, the men's luck had been no better. They'd poked and prodded then knocked to listen for hollow places and finding nothing significant, they were deep in a discussion over a bit of judicious demolition.

Tyler was all for prying off some trim to see what they could see while Finn was firmly against the wanton destruction of perfectly good architectural elements. He called down to Julie from his perch on the staging, "Hey, do you think you're looking for anything metallic? We could rent a metal detector, run it over the area and see if anything triggers."

"Ooh, wait," Gustavia squealed and ran for her bag where after a brief search through its voluminous depths, she pulled out her dowsing rods. "I'm pretty good with these, let me up there, I should be able to get a reading if there's metal."

Finn raised an eyebrow. He'd heard of dowsing but never seen anyone actually do it before.

Gustavia climbed nimbly up the staging and motioned for the men to climb down. It was better if there were no distractions. Grasping one bent rod in each hand, Gustavia raised her arms above shoulder height, aiming them at the flat area just above her head.

At first, she stood still, then she slowly turned in

place. The rods did not move so she lowered them and repeated her actions in another section of the staging. Not a twitch this time, either. "I don't think there's any large amount of metal up here," She called down.

In an undertone, Finn asked, "Do we take that as conclusive evidence?"

Tyler grinned and clapped him on the shoulder, "I do. I've seen her in action."

"Well, okay then. Now what?"

"You're the architectural restoration expert, you tell us." Amethyst pointed a purple tipped finger at Finn.

"I'd say we take a walk through the house looking for other architraves and if we don't find any, then we come back here and rethink. Maybe the—are we calling it treasure? Booty? Loot?" He looked around and since no one answered, continued, "Maybe the valuables aren't metal."

To save energy, Estelle withdrew from Kat leaving the psychic without sight again as they split off into two groups to search the house. Finn leading one, Gustavia—since she knew what to look for—leading the other.

Half an hour later both groups were again clustered around the staging and the mood was grim.

"Clearly we're missing something. Are you sure this is the hiding place? Could it be just another clue?" Finn stepped back to appraise the architrave again.

The architrave spanned the portico over the entrance to the house, resting atop the columns and supporting the frieze, pediment and cornices. If there was any place in that setup to hide something, it was in the pediment, so why had the clue been a solid beam?

Remounting the staging, Finn took a closer look at

the over-sized dentil molding that ran across the face of the architrave. Out of the corner of his eye, he saw Gustavia making the climb to join him. The two stood in comfortable silence for a moment before walking to opposite ends of the staging and prodding each block of the molding in turn, just to see if one of them might trigger something.

"Did you notice there are just twelve blocks to this molding? That leaves ten spaces between. What if..."

Following her train of thought, he reached up to run his fingers along the first space to find a gently curved piece of trim along the lower edge. Something important here, he needed a better look.

Gesturing for Gustavia to follow him, Finn climbed back down and he and Tyler added another section to raise the staging to a height where they could get a full view of the molding.

The foot wide blocks that formed the dentil molding were only spaced about two inches apart. In each space was an additional curved and carved piece of molding with a narrow gap in the back.

Stating the obvious, Tyler said, "These curved spots remind me of the way the lens keys fit into the stained glass windows."

By the time the two of them were back on the ground, Gustavia and Julie were already halfway up the stairs to retrieve the lenses.

After a short discussion, they decided it would be best to pull them from the window in order. Gustavia closed her eyes and brought back the mental image of the window from when the letters glowed.

Picking them off in the order she remembered, she handed them to Julie who stacked them carefully in one hand then returned to the foot of the staging. Since it was Julie's house she joined Finn for the climb back up to place the lenses in the slots and see if anything happened.

When the first lens fit perfectly and settled partway into the slot with an audible click and Julie let out a whoop that nearly caused Finn to jump out of his skin, he lectured her on staging safety but could tell by her unrepentant grin she wasn't listening closely.

"This is it." She called down to the others below then went down the line dropping lenses into place. Click, click, click until finally, there was only one left in her hand. "Ready? Here we go." Julie dropped the final lens into its slot, listened for the click and instead heard a faint whirring sound.

She and Finn looked at each other with identical expressions of surprised consternation. Something had happened but what and where? No sign of anything different on the facade of the portico. Calling down to the others Julie asked, "You see anything from down there?" Shrugs and head shakes were the only answer. They climbed down.

Julius stood watching the activity, an unreadable expression on his face.

Gustavia whirled to confront him, "What now? No wait. Don't tell me." Her eyes narrowed as she fumed in irritation. "Not a lot of help are you?"

"I guess the next logical step is to look around inside." Tyler pointed out the obvious.

"Julie's room first, it's the one behind the portico, seems the most logical place to start." Gustavia determined.

She was the first person through the door and when

she stopped short, Julie nearly slammed into her back. "Whoa."

Gustavia stepped aside making room for the others.

"Well, that's unexpected." Amethyst, always the master of the understatement, intoned.

The lovely crystal chandelier that had previously hung below a decorative medallion in the ceiling was now suspended just a few inches above the floor, the decorative ceiling medallion still attached. Atop the platform it created were several cloth-wrapped bundles.

Looking up through the hole, Tyler pointed to a bit of machinery, "He installed a winch between the ceiling and the floor. The cumulative weight of the lenses must have triggered the switch to activate it. Very clever." He looked over at Julius in appreciation. Julius preened at the attention.

Gustavia looked at Julie and this time the war whoop was expected as they moved together toward the wrapped parcels while Amethyst and Kat moved some things to make a space for them on the desk.

"Wait for us before you open them." Tyler requested then gestured to Finn to follow him out to the portico where they pulled the lenses back out of the slots, retracting the chandelier back into its normal place.

"Handy for cleaning if the switch were more accessible." Finn appreciated the ingenuity. He shook his head, scrubbed a hand over his eyes. "A treasure hunt. Feels a bit surreal."

Figuring it was his right, even if she did have a big bad cop for a brother, Tyler fixed a serious look on his usually cheerful face. "Most valuable treasure you've managed to find is Gustavia. Make sure you appreciate your good fortune. She's one of a kind, Julie's sister in all but blood. That makes her mine. I won't take it kindly if she gets hurt."

Knowing he could choose to be offended, Finn decided, instead, to be thankful the man felt protective, "I've already told Julie this, but I'm not planning on hurting her. I've got my head on square again. Took me long enough to come around but I'm all in. All in, you understand?"

"Yeah, I can see that. Just had to make sure. We've become quite a family, especially the women. Gotta tell you it will be nice to have some more testosterone added to the mix."

"So we're good?"

"As it gets. Not about to speak for the women, though. I expect they'll put you through it a bit before you're fully vetted. I think you can hold your own. Now that we've had our little bonding experience, as Gustavia would call it, let's get back inside and check out the loot."

"Before they're overcome with curiosity, you mean."

"Could happen."

CHAPTER TWENTY-EIGHT

"What's taking them so long?" Gustavia sighed as she absently picked at the cloth covering on one of the packages then gently picked it up and shook it.

"Tyler's giving Finn a "come to Jesus" talk." Amethyst smiled at the thought.

The idea that Tyler would stand for her both dismayed her and made Gustavia feel warm and safe. "Really? You think so?"

"Oh, yeah. He had that look in his eye."

"Surprised it took him this long," Kat said.

"Surprised you didn't have a bet on it." Julie's eyes twinkled while Amethyst rolled hers.

"Hard to bet on something when you're both on the same side of it. Tyler takes his role of our little family patriarch seriously. More every day, I'm thinking. Especially when it comes to you, but I know he'd do the same for me or Kat. He's the best." Julie smiled at that. She fully agreed.

"Here they come." Kat heard them at the foot of the stairs. Finally, they'd get to see what was in the packages. It didn't take her psychic senses or the fact that Estelle was sharing her body to know that the spirits were getting restless at the delay.

Suddenly nervous, when the two men returned to the room, Julie picked up the largest of the cloth bundles and with one last look around at her friends, began removing the outer wrappings. Inside the first layer of coarser cloth was another layer of softer cottony flannel which fell away more easily. Each fold of the cotton, as it unwrapped, revealed a piece of jewelry. Some in soft drawstring bags, some loose, some protected in twists of paper.

Strands of pearls in shades of palest pink to white fell from the folds of cloth as Julie unwound layer after layer. The only noise to be heard was the whispers made by the unwinding cloth punctuated by a softly voiced ooh or ah as each new treasure was revealed.

After the necklaces came matching bracelets, then earrings as she continued deeper into the heart of the packet. Eventually, the last shred of cloth fell away to reveal a small drawstring bag. With shaking hands, Julie untied the knots and pulled open the bag and peeked inside. Wide-eyed, she gestured for Gustavia to hold out her hands then poured a rain of loose pearls into their waiting depths.

Finally, unable to hold it in any longer, Amethyst exclaimed, "Holy cats," and broke the spell making everyone else laugh. She reached into the bounty that Gustavia held and pulled out a perfect specimen, nearly three quarters of an inch in diameter. She rolled it between her fingers; it felt both warm and cool at the same time, almost like a living, breathing thing.

The laughter lightened the mood considerably. The next parcel yielded a much smaller handful of jewelry set with deep, red rubies and another string bag of loose, cut stones. Julie was overwhelmed and passed the final three bundles to her friends to open while the men looked on.

Kat found sapphires; Amethyst, emeralds and Gustavia the cold fire of small, but exquisitely cut diamonds.

If she never bothered with the last two treasures, Julie would have no problem finishing all the repairs the old house needed with plenty left over for a rainy day. It was a lot to take in.

With a sigh, Kat felt Estelle pull her consciousness gently away and a moment later was plunged again into darkness. Someday, sooner rather than later, she hoped that darkness would become a thing of the past. In the meantime, she realized with a start that she felt none of the fear or fatigue that had accompanied the channeling in the past. She was beginning to feel more comfortable with her abilities.

Maybe it was her imagination but each time, the darkness seemed a little less dense. It was hard to tell, though. It might just be wishful thinking.

Estelle joined Julius, both of them beamed proudly, then faded away.

At that point, Finn sat heavily on the foot of Julie's bed. So what if it wasn't manly to feel a bit overwhelmed, it had been quite a day. No wonder these people had such a tight bond. Between this type of experience and dealing with Julie's crazy ex, they couldn't help but become a close knit group.

He looked up to see Amethyst, Gustavia and Tyler looking at him appraisingly. "His aura..." Tyler started to speak. "Wonky does not begin to cover it." Amethyst sounded concerned.

"Trust me, I've got this." Gustavia said confidently. Reaching down, she did nothing more than entwine her fingers with his. He felt it then, the peace that washed over him at her touch. The way the world righted itself.

"Cool." Tyler said as he saw their auras merge then separate; Finn's now clear and vibrant.

Finn stood, pronounced to the room, "I'm going to kiss her now," then followed through. When he let her go, Gustavia had stars in her eyes, ones that shined only for him.

Epilogue

Amethyst sat quietly nearby as Kat laid out the tarot cards. She wasn't using her usual Celtic cross spread this time. Nor was she using her mythic deck.

No, this time she was using a set of cards she never used with clients. This deck had been handmade by her grandmother to probe into darker, deeper mysteries. When it had been passed on to Kat, it had been with the understanding that this deck and its companion layout was for emergencies only.

Since Logan's reappearance several weeks before, she'd been having vividly visual dreams, the kind she'd had as a child, before her gift had become active. At first they'd been harmless, fairytale-like and she'd enjoyed them but as the days passed, she began to sense an amorphous presence. One that created enough fear to turn her bones liquid and leave her feeling powerless.

This spread was her last ditch effort. Kat needed to get to the root of the problem; this spread should help her plumb the depths of her subconscious. At least she hoped so. The figure was becoming clearer and more menacing with every appearance.

Telling Amethyst about her dreams hadn't been easy

but, since her friend had the uncanny ability to read auras, there was no sense in trying to hide the problem. So, Kat had confided and now Amethyst was there to provide support and because she was, the cards included her in their revelation.

Amethyst was about to get a surprise. Too bad Kat couldn't tell if it would be a good one or a bad one.

Seven cards made up the spread and as each one fell, her dread increased. The situation with Logan was more complicated than she'd thought. Pure evil had a hold on him. The same evil she'd begun to see in her dreams and she was afraid that if that figure ever got close enough to see her in return, she and her friends would never be safe again.

The End.